A horse, a boy, and a

MIRACLE OF LOVE

Published by Promise Press, an imprint of Barbour Publishing, Inc., P.O. Box 719, Uhrichsville, Ohio 44683, www.promisepress.com

Member of the
Evangelical Christian
Publishers Association

Printed in the United States of America.
5 4 3 2 1

the gift

A horse, a boy, and a

MIRACLE OF LOVE

L A U R A I N E
S N E L L I N G

PROMISE PRESS

An Imprint of Barbour Publishing

o n e

"Cody, old horse, you look as lonely as I feel."

Cody raised his head from the water trough and, his lower lip hanging loose as always, he dribbled water on Turner McNeally's down vest.

"Boy, you sure could use a brushing." Turner flipped the water droplets off his front and rubbed the leopard Appaloosa's dirty white ears. "Dani would be on my case like you going after the last kernel of grain in the feed box."

Cody snorted, sending smaller droplets in the direction of Mac's face. Turner had lived most of his forty-two years known by the handle of Mac. He'd never cared for Turner, renaming himself even before he went to grade school. He drew a red print handkerchief from his back pocket and wiped his face, brushing the water off his mustache, which matched his silver-flecked, sealskin brown hair. His daughter, Danielle, now away at college, teased him about the silver, telling him he looked distinguished.

"You about done or do I get another bath?"

Cody rubbed his forehead against Mac's shoulder, leaving behind a sprinkle of white hairs on the red and black plaid flannel shirt. When the horse paused in his rubbing, Mac took the hint and scratched the broad plate between the horse's eyes.

"You know, sometimes I get so I could drive clear to Chicago just to see her." *Or bring her back.* He never could figure out why a country girl like his Dani would choose a big city college like Northwestern. Of course, it might have had something to do with the full scholarship they'd offered her. Danielle was not only pure grace on the basketball floor, she had a mind that considered physics child's play and quantum physics pure fascination.

"Couldn't stand in her way, now could we?"

Cody shook his head, both ears and lower lip flopping in the process. He nudged Mac again, a tad more firmly this time. After all, the fingers had ceased their motion, and the man had yet to stroke the black-dotted neck.

"All right, I get the point." Mac took up stroking again, wincing at the cloud of dust and loose hair that followed his hand. *Danielle. My Dani.* How the light had gone out of his life after seeing her get on that plane at Los Angeles International Airport. It was almost as bad as when they notified him that his wife and son had been killed in a traffic pileup on Highway 58, down by Caliente. Well, not really, at least he'd see Dani before summer, God willing. He'd never taken good-byes for granted again, and ten years passing didn't make them any easier. Nowhere had he read a guarantee that you would see someone you loved again after you said good-bye. Now he always said, "I'll see you," and he knew that to be true, whether here or in heaven. Only God knew which.

"Come along, Boy, let's get you cleaned up and then I gotta go check on the cows." He headed for the barn, the horse tagging along as he always did, his nose bumping the man's elbow every few steps, as if to remind him he wasn't alone.

After brushing the horse and pouring a can of feed in the black rubber tub in the manger, Mac carefully locked the gate behind him and headed for the truck. Driving out to the west pasture was easier than walking. Riding Cody would have done them both some good, but the truck was faster. Not that he was in a hurry or anything. He checked the float in the round stock tank, scooped out a couple handfuls of floating green algae, and counted the cows with their calves that grazed the ten-acre pasture. *About time to switch them to the next section.* If only the rains would come so he didn't have to move the irrigation pipes again. While winter had come to much of the country, fall hung on here in the Tehachapi Mountains of California.

Back at the house, on the rear deck overlooking the wooded hills that rose from Cummins Valley, he automatically kicked the dust off his boots at the bootjack by the back door before he entered the darkened family room. *If you don't like the dark, you can't blame anyone but yourself,* he scolded himself. *You'd think by now you'd remember to leave a light on.* He flipped the light switch, ignoring the sorrow that still knifed through his soul and caught him unawares, even after all these years. As he knew by now, it would go away and sometimes the joy of their time together would sneak up and comfort him. He seemed to have no control over either.

Since Danielle, who'd become an excellent cook, left for school, he had decreed cooking a waste of time. He often made a large pot of something on Saturday and when he got tired of eating it, bagged the leftovers and threw the bags in the freezer. Each night, he took out whatever looked good and, within minutes, the microwave had his dinner hot. He'd rather read than cook any day—unless he had the pleasure of cooking for company.

Tonight he chose stew. When the oven *dinged,* he took his bowl to the table and wrote out an ad to run in the local paper. *The Tehachapi News,* unlike many weeklies, was worth reading.

Old horse needs young companion. He crossed it out and started again.

Old horse lonely.
Needs young companion.
Not for sale.
Not forever.
Just for fun.

He eyed the form and half-shrugged. Not bad and it would attract more attention in free form than straight paragraph. "Lord, You know what I need. What Cody needs. Surely You have just the perfect kid in mind. Boy, girl, doesn't matter, but someone who needs us, too." He scrubbed his forehead with callused fingertips. "Good thing I can talk out loud to You or someone coming in would think I've gone round the bend."

Bungee, the cow dog with one blue eye, one marbled, rose from his place beside Mac and laid his head on the man's thigh.

"You think that?" Mac stroked the gray, black, brown,

and silver mottled fur and read over his ad again. Bungee only whimpered deep in his throat. "Well, Lord, unless You have something better in mind, I'll turn this in tomorrow morning on my way to the Miller job." He glanced at the calendar. To meet his bid, he only had three days left to finish the rough-in phase of the plumbing on the house in progress. "Should make that." He stroked the dog's head again and, using both hands, fluffed Bungee's ears and rubbed his thumbs down the sides of the dog's face. "I imagine you want to eat, too."

Bungee brushed the aging hardwood floor with his fluffy bit of a tail and whined again.

Mac read the ad one more time. "Just for fun." He nodded. "Sure as I'm sitting here, I hope it will be."

two

"I'm sorry, Mrs. Wilkinson, I wish I could offer you some hope."

"You did. You said there is no physical reason why Jonah doesn't talk." Rebecca Wilkinson refused to use the word *can't*. Not that she believed her eight-year-old son chose not to talk but. . . She nodded and sighed simultaneously, then forced her knees to do their job and help her get upright. At the moment legs, joints, mind, all felt like jellyfish looked. They'd been given that name for a reason. Rebecca pasted on a professional smile and held out her hand. "Thank you for being so good with him."

"I just wish I could say and do more." Winsome Amy Cartwright, who looked more like a high school gymnast than an accredited speech therapist, turned with Rebecca to looked through the one-way glass to watch the boy.

Small for his age, his dark hair was cut so it fell straight from a center spot. The tip of his tongue peeked between rosy lips. His dark eyes matched those of his father's. He leaned forward, meticulously coloring in the last picture he'd drawn for the therapist. A mommy, a little boy, and a daddy with no head. The male figure always wore a green uniform, indicative of the U.S. Army.

Rebecca sometimes wondered if her son was forgetting his father. Anymore, Jonah seldom shed tears when he held the picture of U.S. Major Gordon K. Wilkinson—missing in action but later found dead, possibly a casualty of friendly fire in war-torn Bosnia. But Jonah's detail-rich drawing, even down to the epaulets on his dad's shoulders, convinced Rebecca that her son's memories of his father had survived.

She stared through the glass as if, by concentrating hard enough, she could will her son to talk—to return to the laughing, chattering child of his first four years of life. . .

. . .Jonah, whose father lifted him to touch the ceiling, both of them chuckling a belly laugh, one baritone, one soprano, a perfect blend of joy.

. . .Jonah, a fist full of angleworms rushing back outside to loose them in the garden soil when she gently told him they needed dirt to live.

. . .Jonah and Gordon watching a spider spin a web and cheering when the spider trapped a fly.

She leaned her forehead against the glass, her fingers spread, palm flat against the cool surface. *Jonah, how can I help you?*

Rebecca turned at the gentle pressure on her shoulder, wiping her eyes with her fingertips.

"I have a suggestion for you—well, a couple of suggestions, in fact. I'm glad you are mainstreaming him. He is hard to place since he spoke at one time, but putting him with the autistic or hearing-impaired kids will be a disaster. Did you try teaching him to sign? Some classes are learning sign as part of the curriculum—" Dr. Cartwright flipped the pages in a notebook on her desk before shaking her head. "—But none of them in Tehachapi. Sorry."

"I took him to a class once, and he sat there with his hands clenched under his arms. The look on his face made it real clear he would have none of it. I suppose we could try again now that he is a bit older."

"My next suggestion is a pet. Many times animals can reach a heart and actually make the owner healthier."

Rebecca knew she'd been shaking her head through the entire last line, if not on the outside, for sure on the inside. "We live in an apartment that doesn't allow pets, at least not dogs and cats."

"What about a rat or a bunny, something that likes to be cuddled."

"I–I'll think about it." Rebecca kept her aversion to critters with naked tails to herself. "Can rabbits be housebroken?"

"Oh, yes, quite easily. Birds like a cockatiel or parakeet are a possibility, too, but they don't cuddle quite as well."

"Looks like I better be searching for a house sooner than I thought. My plan was to rent for six months to a year and see how we like it up here before plunking the money down on a house." She turned back to the window. "But if a pet would help, I'd do it." *I'll do anything to bring Jonah back to himself.*

"If you could, something to keep in mind, as far as I've observed, the larger animals are more helpful."

"Larger than dogs and cats?" At the therapist's nod, Rebecca could feel her brow furrowing. "You mean horses, cows, that sort of thing?"

"If you can. Are you an animal lover yourself?"

"I don't know. I'm an army brat, and my father said no pets since we moved around so much. Then I married a career officer, and I guess I assumed the no-pet rule still held." She let her hands fall to her side. "And after Gordon was killed, I–I just had to get through it."

Jonah quit talking, and I started running. What a wounded pair we are.

"If you get a place where you can have a dog, check out the animal shelters, either down in Mojave or in Bakersfield. There are some good dogs or cats there who need loving homes."

Nodding, Rebecca, picked up her purse. "Thank you, I will." She extended her hand. "And thank you for your help. If you locate a signing class, I'd appreciate it if you would let me know." She followed the therapist to the door and entered the playroom. "Time to go, Sport." She took his jacket off the peg and held it for him to slip into, then knelt to join the zipper slide and zip it up. "You better wear your hat; it's cold out there."

After handing Jonah her purse, Rebecca shrugged into her cream and green polar fleece jacket. The stately pine trees that bordered the jacket reminded her of the last place she'd really called *home*—Fort Lewis in the state of Washington, where towering fir trees shaded their backyard. She and Gordon had loved Washington's primeval forest. But that was several moves ago, before the high desert of Tehachapi, where the wind that ran the windmills on the eastern ridges also tried to steal hats and jackets. She reached for Jonah's hand, ignoring the look of resentment in his eyes.

"Don't want you blown clear across the valley." One thing she'd learned since moving here: The wind seldom took a vacation.

Back in their two-bedroom apartment, located on the second floor as a safety measure, she hung up their jackets, nodded when Jonah pointed toward the television, and ambled into the red and white kitchen to fix them a snack before starting dinner. Slicing some cheddar cheese, she put it along with Ritz crackers on two red glass plates and took them into the living room. She placed one by Jonah, who lay on his belly on the floor, feet in the air, crossing and recrossing at the ankles. The only time some part of Jonah was not moving was when he was asleep.

He smiled his thanks.

"You're welcome." Taking her snack to Gordon's dark leather recliner, she curled up with the stack of mail and *The Tehachapi News*. Since most of the mail went directly into the round file, she put the two bills to one side and read the postcard from a friend playing in the waves of Hawaii. She couldn't help but drool over the unbelievably blue water her friend said was really that color. *Someday,* she promised herself as she set the card on top of the bills. *Someday we're going there, too.*

She read the headlines on the front page, flipping through until she found Jon Hammond's nature column. While she read, she chuckled over his descriptions of deer mice. *He makes even me, a virulently anti-rodent woman, want to watch them. From a distance, of course.* She read the local wit's column, the lines under the pictures, skipped the athletic news, and ended at the ads. After perusing the houses for sale, a boxed poem caught her eye under the *Animal* column.

Old horse lonely.
Needs young companion.
Not for sale.
Not forever.
Just for fun.

The phone number at the bottom seemed to blink in flashing neon lights.

A horse? He's too little to ride a horse. A pony perhaps—but a horse? She glanced over at her son, who was dividing his attention between a rerun of *The Andy Griffith Show* on television and a book on dinosaurs open in front of him. Jonah never had liked the commercials.

Had he always been so solitary? Were there no children who called him *friend* or who he played with at school? Surely he was not the only new kid in the third grade this year? After all, at parent/teacher night, Miss

17

Swenson said he was doing well. Did that mean socially as well as academically? She'd been so relieved at the news, she'd forgotten to ask about friends.

Rebecca turned her attention back to the ad in the paper. *Old horse needs companionship.* The therapist had said an animal might help Jonah. Could this be a match? Surely an old horse would be plenty tame and gentle.

She closed her eyes. *If anything happens to Jonah—God in heaven, You couldn't be so cruel again. Could You?*

three

*M*cNeally here."

"I'm calling in response to the ad in *The Tehachapi News* about an old horse needing a young companion?"

"That's me." *Lady, I'm not going to eat you, loosen up.* Mac leaned back in his brown leather recliner, the cordless phone clamped between ear and shoulder. One hand found its way to rub Bungee's ears while he smoothed his mustache with the other.

"Ah, could you tell me something about the horse? I mean, my son has never been near a horse before."

Poor kid. "Sure, Cody is my daughter's horse, and with her off to college, he needs a friend. He's gentle, wouldn't hurt a fly. . . ." *Now that's one of the stupidest things to say. Of course he'd hurt a fly. He'd kill the pesky things if he could catch 'em.* "I mean, he's really good with people of all ages, but kids especially. Dani, that's my daughter, used to work him with handicapped kids in the local program." *Talk about running off at the mouth. . .* Mac shook his head. *You'd think I never had anyone to talk to.* "How old is your boy?"

"Eight, but he's small for his age. Third grade."

"Well, if you'd like to bring him on out, we can see how they go together."

"Could you tell me the charge, please?"

"Charge? Lady, you'd be doing me a favor."

"Oh. But—I mean, like I said, Jonah has never been around horses. . . ."

"Don't worry, I'll be there to show him what he needs to know."

"And. . . " The pause stretched. "You–you wouldn't leave him alone—with the horse, I mean."

Mac rolled his eyes. What kind of an idiot did she think he was? No one left an eight-year-old kid alone with a strange animal, especially a child with no experience. "Do you have a pencil and paper? I'll give you directions. We're easy to find."

"Just a minute."

He could hear her rustling around, a television playing in the background. So Jonah was eight, one year older than Tim when the accident happened. Strange how he still dated everything from before and after the accident that changed his life.

"Okay, sorry for the delay, I'm ready."

"Where are you coming from?"

"The apartments on Valley Boulevard."

"Okay, stay on Valley, it becomes 202, take that until you turn right on Cummins Valley Road, take that to Banducci and turn left. You'll see my sign, McNeally's Plumbing, on the right. Just follow the drive right on up to the house. You'll see Cody out in the pasture. Don't be afraid of the dog. He's all bark. When would you like to come?"

"What about tomorrow after three? That's when school is out."

Mac checked his calendar. "I can be here by three-thirty." While he said the words, he mentally computed all that had to go right on the job for him to get home on time. His helper could finish up whatever he didn't get done—at least he hoped his helper could do that. It all depended on whether or not he showed up for work. "May I have your name and phone number in case something accidentally comes up?"

"Oh, I'm sorry. My name is Rebecca Wilkinson." She gave him her phone number, too, and after the good-byes, they hung up.

Mac stared at the phone. Strange and interesting all

at the same time. Why did he have a feeling that something was wrong with the boy? All she'd said was he—What was his name? Mac closed his eyes to think better and run the conversation through again. *Ah, Jonah, that's it.* All she'd said was he was eight years old and small for his age. Oh, and that he'd never been around horses.

Bungee yipped at his knee and, placing both paws in Mac's lap, stared into his eyes.

"It's okay, Boy. In fact, tomorrow you will be delighted. A boy is coming to visit." Mac ruffled the dog's fluffy ears and rocked his head from side to side. "I wonder if his mother, Rebecca. . ." He tasted her name on his tongue. " . . .If she will want to stay and watch? Sometimes kids do better without a parent around, at least at first."

Bungee whined, but Mac deflected the tongue that aimed for his nose and let it kiss his hand instead.

By two the next afternoon, Mac knew he was in trouble. In fact, he'd known it by noon. Randy, his helper, showed up late with some cockamamie excuse. The electrician wanted to get going early. The owner of the house decided to add a commode and sink in the laundry room. And his favorite drill motor went AWOL.

When he tried the phone number Rebecca had

given him, the machine clicked on, so he had no idea if she got his message or not. By the time he drove up the driveway, four o'clock had come and gone. He thought spitting nails sounded like a welcome relief.

A blue SUV waited in the turnaround. Bungee left his self-assigned place beside the driver's door and bounded over to Mac's three-quarter-ton pickup, loaded with work boxes, pipe racks, and one irate driver.

He parked by the SUV and climbed out, slapping the dust off his jeans and retrieving his felt Western hat from the bench seat. By the time he came around the end of the truck bed, his guests had climbed out of the SUV. Mac extended his hand. "Sorry to be late. I sure hope you got my message and just arrived."

"No. We've been waiting since three-thirty." Rebecca shook hands with him, all the while keeping a wary eye on the dog, who wagged himself into a frenzy. "I'm Rebecca Wilkinson and this is Jonah." Her other hand kept her son on the opposite side of her, well away from the dog.

"Sorry I'm late. It's been one of those days. I'm Turner McNeally, but I go by Mac." He shifted his attention to the boy. "Jonah, this is Bungee, and that wriggling rear of his and laughing face should tell you he can't wait to make your acquaintance."

"I wasn't sure. I mean, I don't know much about dogs, so I didn't dare get out of the car."

"I see. You can pet him. He's got a lightning tongue, but he'd never bite. He likes his ears rubbed." Mac smiled at the boy with brown eyes who reminded him of the big-eyed children portrayed in popular art some years before. "Bungee, sit." The dog sat, his bit of fluff tail whisking the ground and his front feet beating a tattoo on the gravel.

Jonah looked from the dog to his mother and, at her nod, stepped forward. He laid a tentative hand on Bungee's head and earned a clean chin for his efforts. Taking two steps back, he again eye-checked with his mother, scrubbed at his chin, and slowly raised his hand back to the dog's head.

Mac watched the boy and the dog, all the while conscious of the woman. Worry or fear pinched her eyes and ridged her wide forehead. If she wasn't careful, she wouldn't have any lower lip left. And her hands, lovely hands with long fingers, hadn't caught a still moment since she'd shaken his hand. He'd forgotten how soft a woman's hands could be—soft skin, but with a firm handshake. However, her wide-set eyes struck him the most. Her dark lashes shielded amber pupils with gold flecks that had lost their sparkle. He had observed them with a momentary scan, but they left the imprint of a red-hot branding iron.

"Mr. McNeally?" Her voice seemed a matching brand—rich, like warm cream—yet with a hesitancy that brought out whatever protective instincts he had left over from caring for Danielle.

"Ah, yes. Shall we go meet Cody?" *McNeally, where is your head? Get with the program before she thinks you're some kind of dodo.* Flashes of a young Danielle, laughing at the word *dodo* and giving it intonations from high to low to deep bass, interfered with his view of the two beside him.

Concentrate, Man. The inner voice went from teasing to drill sergeant orders.

"Nice place you have here."

"Thanks." —*Oh, man of few words,* he thought with a snicker.

"Be careful, Jonah. You might trip on those rocks."

Mac turned enough to see her reach for her son, who had, totally boylike, jumped from one to another of the flat rocks that lined the path. The boy flashed her a smile, but when he caught Mac looking at them, he stepped off the six-inch high rocks and walked close enough to his mother to make her put a hand on his shoulder. *Something strange is going on here.*

"How do you like school?" Mac asked.

Jonah smiled again, this time with a slight shrug.

"Who's your teacher?"

"Miss Swenson," Rebecca answered.

Why don't you let him answer? But, as they reached the fence, Mac held back from voicing his response and whistled for Cody. "This is Cody, my daughter Danielle's horse. He's a leopard Appaloosa, used to be pretty good on the barrels, and he's still a great trail horse."

"Barrels? Trail horse?"

Oh, a real city slicker. "Danielle ran Cody in barrel racing, a highly competitive event. Trail horse refers to riding up in the mountains or hills, anywhere there might be trails instead of corrals or open fields. They competed in trail-riding competitions also."

"Are you sure a horse with that kind of training would be safe for a little boy?"

"I'm sure, but you can see for yourself." Mac dug in his vest pocket to see if there were any horse treats left. He found two and gave Jonah one. "Here, I'll show you how, and you can give Cody a treat. He likes this about as much as you like candy."

Jonah took it in his hand, but his eyes gave him away. Flat-out fear. Why should he be afraid if he's never had anything to do with horses? Mac knew his questions were stacking up like firewood for the winter.

Cody trotted up, his lower lip bobbling, mane flopping, and his ears pricked forward. Cody liked treats, but he also liked kids. He arched his neck over the rail that rode the top of the fence posts and whuffled, his nostrils fluttering in the near-silent greeting.

"You hold your hand out flat with the treat on your palm. See the way I'm doing it?" Mac pushed Cody's nose away from the treat. "You want to keep your fingers stretched out like this so he doesn't mistake them for something to eat."

At the woman's swift intake of breath and the boy's step backward, Mac realized he'd just said the wrong thing. "Not that Cody would bite you. He's really wiser than that, but I want to teach you good habits right from the beginning."

Cody stretched out and nuzzled Mac's shoulder.

"See, he likes treats and he can smell we have some." Mac held his hand flat and set the tan biscuit in the center of his palm. "Like this. Show me yours." The boy did exactly as Mac showed. "Good. Now I'll give him mine first so you see how gentle he is." Hoping the woman got the hint also, Mac held out his hand. Cody lipped the treat and crunched, the sound loud in the stillness, as if both boy and mother were holding their breath. *I should have one to give her to try, too, kill that fear thing*

27

the gift

before it gets out of hand.

Cody tossed his head and nudged Mac's shoulder.

"See, he wants more. Your turn now." He kept his hand on the long bones of Cody's nose to slow down the interaction. "Good." The boy held his hand flat like he'd been shown, treat in place, and extended it to the horse. "Good. Okay, Cody, help yourself."

Dainty as a parasoled lady taking tea, Cody lifted the biscuit with barely a whiskery lip brush against Jonah's palm. The boy's eyes flew wide open. He rubbed the center of his hand with his fingers and beamed up at Mac, his round face reflecting the sun that would soon be behind the hills. He grinned at his mother, too, and took his first step closer to Mac.

When Cody's nostrils fluttered again, the boy looked up at the man beside him. Questions covered his face.

"That's his way of asking for more. Dani, my daughter, called it 'Cody talk.' He can nicker, which is a friendly sound; neigh, which can be much louder; and whinny, the loudest." Mac decided not to mention the scream of a stallion or a horse in pain. At times, some things were better left unsaid. *Why isn't he asking the questions I can see all over him? Is he that shy? Must be it.* Mac looked at the boy's mother, who had eyes only for her son.

"Would you like to pet him?"

28

Jonah flashed his mother another of those permission looks before nodding.

"Cody likes to be petted, here around his ears, down on his neck, his cheeks, and down his nose." Mac indicated each area as he said the name. "He likes firm petting, otherwise he thinks you are tickling him or might be a fly." Demonstrating long smooth strokes, Mac waited for the boy to gain his courage. Finally Jonah stepped closer to the man and reached to the side of Cody's head. His smile widened as he patted the horse, first tentatively, then with more firmness, mimicking Mac perfectly.

"Would you like to learn to brush him? Cody's in bad need of a good brushing."

Again, that quick look for permission before nodding. Mac followed the boy's glance to see Rebecca with her shoulders hunched, hands in her jacket pockets. She looked about to duck before she was struck by a blow.

"I'll show you where we keep the grooming equipment. Dani took over part of the feed room as her tack room." At the questioning look, Mac added, "Tack is what we call the saddle, saddle blanket, and bridle." *This kid doesn't miss a thing. Wonder what he'd be like without his mother along. Is she so strict with him that he can't speak for himself?*

"I'm afraid we can't stay much longer. It'll be dark soon."

"Oh, okay. Maybe we should put off the brushing until another day. Jonah, how would you like to measure the grain for Cody instead?" *Lady, we do have electricity out here.*

After the usual glance toward his mother, Jonah nodded.

Mac led the way to the feed barrel, lifted the lid, and handed Cody the plastic scoop. "Fill that about half full. You can stand on that block of wood, and I'll show you where to dump it. Cody will be there waiting."

Jonah scooped out mixed grain, eyed it, and dumped some back, giving Mac one of those questioning looks that earned him a nod and a smile. He followed Mac to the rear of the barn, where the horse came through an open, sliding door into a shavings-carpeted stall with two-by-sixes for the bars. Cody nickered, very clearly demanding his feed. Mac pointed to a wooden manger set in the wall, and Jonah dumped the feed in.

"Good job, Jonah." Mac clapped him on the shoulder, and the two headed back for the tack room, where Rebecca waited, arms now crossed against the chill or with trepidation. Mac wasn't sure which. *If she was so worried, why didn't she come along?*

As they left the barn and headed for the cars, she sighed. "Thank you, Mr. McNeally. We appreciate your time and assistance." Formality seemed part of her ingrained suit of armor.

The thought fit with his earlier assessment.

"Mac, remember?"

"Okay. When would it be all right for us to come again?"

He'd been half-expecting her to say good-bye and thanks for the effort—but this was enough. "I'd like to say tomorrow, but this job I'm on is having some problems. So would Saturday be all right? Say around ten?"

She paused for a moment, then nodded. "We'll see you at ten."

Mac, with Bungee at his side, watched them raise a dust cloud down the drive, not a hard thing to do, dry as it was. "Bungee, there's something strange here. How long, you think, before she lets me in on the secret?"

four

"Did you like that?"

Jonah's face lit up the car. His nod set his bangs to bobbing.

"Good."

Now to call Mr. McNea—Mac, Rebecca corrected herself, *to explain things.* Now to quiet her deeply buried secret wish that Jonah would have said something to the horse or the man or the dog. She'd hardly been aware of the wish, but any little change in their lives always triggered the dream, which inevitably wormed its way through all her barriers and defenses. Sometimes, she wished she had the kind of faith Gordon had had; but if he was right, he was celebrating now. She took her faith out, dusted it off for Christmas and Easter, and then, in spite of good intentions, let other things bury it securely back in its box.

Would that help me any with the loneliness?

Forget that, Kid. You just keep putting one foot in front of the other, and you'll come out all right in the end. She could hear her father's voice as plain as if he were sitting right beside her.

Back in their apartment, when Jonah started on his homework, she went to her bedroom/office, picked up the phone, and checked the phone number she'd written on the pad she kept handy. Wishing she were somewhere else wouldn't help, so she obeyed her father's strictures to get the worst over with first. Then, the rest would be easier. Easier yet might have been telling Mr. McNe—no, Mac, face to face, so she could see his reactions. Would he think less of her son? Might he cancel the arrangements because he couldn't handle someone different? But then, he said his daughter took Cody to be ridden by handicapped kids. Surely she'd learned that kind of caring from her father. Or her mother. If she had a mother, why hadn't she come out when they sat waiting in the car for Mac to return? Or perhaps they were divorced or she had a job that kept her late.

Get with it! Rebecca sat at her desk and dialed the phone with a sigh.

"McNeally here."

"Hi, Mac, this is Rebecca Wilkinson."

"Well, hello." The warm timbre of his voice sent a shiver up her back.

"I want to thank you for taking the time with Jonah."

"You already did."

"Oh." *Come back, Brain, where did you go?* "Yes, well, there's something I have to tell you."

"All right."

"It—it's about Jonah. I know you are wondering why he never answered your questions. . . ."

"I thought maybe he was mighty shy."

"No, he doesn't talk." There. She'd said it.

"Oh?"

"Not since his father was killed in the military."

"Ah."

"Jonah was four; and after we had the funeral, he never said another word." She swallowed as the tears, which still came so easily at times, burned her eyes, and flooded her throat and nose.

"Poor kid."

"Yeah. They say there is nothing physically wrong, but some switch flipped in his brain. We keep hoping something will throw it back the other way. I just wanted to tell you so. . ."

"So. . . ?"

"So." She heaved a sigh. "So you won't think he's weird or something."

"I'd say in spite of his tragedy, he's a bright and observant child."

"Oh." She rolled her eyes toward the ceiling to try to stave off fresh tears. *Kick me or yell at me and I'll deal with it, but be nice to me and I fall apart.* "Thanks. We'll see you on Saturday. Bye." She dropped the phone on the desk and after snagging three tissues from the box by the lamp, she buried her face in them and let the tears flow. She fought to cry silently, but even so, she felt a small hand on her shoulder. "D–don't worry, Sport, I guess I just need a good cry. I'll be all right in a few moments." As the sobs subsided, like she knew they would, she thought back to the phone call. How rude she'd been to cut him off like that. Now he must think she was weird. Or a crybaby. Or—or— She shook her head and blew her nose. Better get dinner going. Tonight was broiled chicken night, thighs for her, drumsticks for Jonah, along with macaroni and cheese, one of their favorite meals.

He was happiest if she didn't try to force the vegetables' issue. Just like his father. So many things about her son reminded her of Gordon. The cleft in his chin, the way he turned to look at her when he was worried, the color and shape of his eyes, his curiosity that never took a moment off. If only he could talk.

She spent the evening catching up on the backlog of work for her clients. One good thing about bookkeeping, thanks to the computer and Internet: She could live anywhere and still keep her clients. They sent her their receipts and account information; she did the work and e-mailed the finished product.

Saturday morning, Jonah was up, dressed, had eaten his Cap'n Crunch, made his bed, and put his laundry in the basket before his mother wandered into the kitchen, dreaming of hot coffee served instantly.

"Did you eat?"

He nodded and showed her his cereal bowl in the dishwasher, along with her cup from the night before.

She yawned and stretched, then filled the coffee maker with water and vanilla-flavored grind and plugged it in. "Why I don't fix this the night before and set the timer, I'll never know." She turned to ask Jonah something and realized he'd gone to watch cartoons. A note on the table in large block letters said 9:30 A.M. She smiled at the reminder. No doubt on that score, Jonah wanted to go out to see Cody again. While the coffee dripped, she went back to her room, glancing into Jonah's to see the bed made and floor neat. *Taking no chances, is he?*

She made her own bed, waiting for the *bing* from the liquid energy maker.

By the time they drove into the McNeally yard, they were still ten minutes early; and, if Jonah had had his way, they'd have been half an hour earlier. Bungie greeted them with deep-throated barks and a bouncing lope that gave him his name. When Jonah opened his car door, the dog sniffed once, then turned himself inside out to greet him.

"Be careful, Jonah, he doesn't know you that well yet." Her caution was lost in the yipping.

Mac came out the back door, shrugging into his sheepskin vest over a blue plaid flannel shirt. He looked just as good in daylight as he had in her dream. She'd read once about warm-fudge eyes. The description fit. Chiseled jaw, too, but the rough edges were softened by smile lines bracketing his mouth and crinkling the edges of those eyes.

Stop it, she warned herself. *You're here to help your son, not to dream of cowboys, nor a certain cowboy, if one could call a plumber a cowboy.* But then how many plumbers wore a sweat-darkened tan Western hat with the edges slightly rolled up, worn jeans with a tooled belt and an engraved oval belt buckle, and a sheepskin vest?

"Good morning." He smiled at each of them, making eye contact at the same time.

The flutter she felt in her middle hadn't made itself known since Gordon died.

"How about we give Cody a good brushing and then I teach you how to saddle him up?" He looked at Jonah, who bobbed his head. His smile said all the words he couldn't utter.

I want to learn, too. Rebecca kept her words to herself. *This is for Jonah's benefit,* she had to remind herself a second time. She followed behind the two of them, distancing herself.

"And then we'll put Cody on a lunge line. That's a long rope, and you can ride him around the corral."

"He's never ridden before, remember? Let's not rush things." *Be careful with my son,* her mind screamed.

Mac stopped and slowly turned to look at her, one eyebrow cocking in a way that clearly said, *You think I don't know what I am doing?* "He'll be all right. I'll be at the other end of the lunge line and keep it short until I feel certain he is secure."

"Oh." Talk about being chastised with a look and gentle words.

Mac whistled and, down in the field, Cody raised his head. When Mac whistled again, the horse broke into a trot, his mane flying in the breeze.

"Oh, he's so beautiful." Indeed, the lightly spotted

white horse, which galloped across the pasture, looked like a movie rendition of wild mustang days.

"Doesn't look old when he runs that way, does he? — Not that twenty is old for a horse, but he's no youngster anymore, either." Mac slapped Cody's neck and raised a cloud of dust. The horse appeared to take the move as one of affection. The horse sniffed the man's pockets, then nuzzled one, and nudged the laughing owner. "Can't fool you, can I?" Mac pulled out two horse cookies and gave one to Jonah before giving the other to Cody. "Now it's your turn; remember to keep your hand flat."

Jonah did as he was told and giggled, rubbing his hand after Cody whiskered it, lifting his treat.

Rebecca swallowed the rising "Be careful" and wished she could feel the horse's whiskery lips on her hand. Or was she thinking of another kind of whiskers brushing her palm? She swallowed again, this time hoping the heat she felt rising from her neck might somehow be attributed to the weather.

"Okay, Jonah, let's go back to the barn. Cody will meet us there." They turned as one, with Rebecca tagging along behind, and ambled back to the hip-roofed barn with a stone foundation that looked like it had sprouted right out of the land.

"You get the bucket of brushes out of the tack room,

and I'll let Cody in through the back door." Mac pointed to the tack room and watched while Jonah scampered off to do his bidding. He flashed Rebecca a smile and continued on into the dimness of the dirt-floored building.

She leaned against the open door. "Good job, Jonah." Her son's grin caught at her heart. How unlike him to take to a stranger as quickly as he had to Mac. Was it the pull of the horse or the man himself?

Down at the end of the barn, the door squealed as Mac pushed it open and let Cody in. He grabbed the horse by the mane and put some kind of harness over his head, then buckled it behind the ears. Taking a rope off the hook on the wall, he snapped that under the horse's chin and the two walked together, Cody's head bobbing along about the man's elbow, keeping time with Mac's feet.

Rebecca rubbed her elbows. The chill of the sharp breeze bit through her jacket. One thing about Tehachapi: It did have four seasons just as the advertisement promised. Or was it the disconcerting chill of being out of her comfort zone? A horse, a barn, her son trying new things.

"This is a halter. This is a lead rope or shank. I'm going to tie this other end to that round metal circle on the post there. You see that?" Jonah nodded. "We always tie Cody up like that when we groom him so that if something spooks him, he won't run off. Not that much spooks old Cody here, but it is wise to be careful. What you learn with one horse, you'll know for all the others."

Jonah's quick smile brought one in return.

"I believe if you learn things right in the beginning, life gets plenty easier later on." As he talked, Mac stroked the horse and reached for one of the brushes. "Now, this one is good for general brushing. See how stiff the bristles are?" He scrubbed them across his hand, the sound like dry leaves rattling in the wind. "The other one there is softer, for his face. And that black rubber oval is a curry and good for cleaning off mud or pulling out dead hair in the spring. Now, since he is so dirty, which one should I use?"

Jonah handed him the curry.

"Good. Now, since I have two hands, I will use the curry in one and the stiff brush in the other. Grooming is a two-handed job, goes much faster this way." He stroked down Cody's shoulder, the curry hand followed by the brush hand. "There is another brush in there that you can use, and you just follow what I'm doing."

He let Jonah brush a few times and then handed him the curry. "Now you can do it right. You start with his neck and shoulder, go on to his belly, and then his rump. Don't use the curry down on his legs, but it's good for the mane, all that long hair on his neck."

Jonah's forehead wrinkled in his concentration as he brushed.

"I think we'll have to get you a box to stand on, but this time I'll do the high parts. See, short strokes like this loosen the dirt and dig it out."

All the while Mac talked and brushed, he pointed out things like following the way of the hair, the flank where Cody was ticklish, and how watching the ears told them what Cody was thinking.

He couldn't be thinking much, Rebecca thought, *he's almost asleep.* She shivered.

"You want to come help?"

Rebecca started. "Me?"

"Who else?"

"I guess."

"After all, Jonah might want a horse of his own someday, and you'll need to know all this stuff, too. My Dani got her first horse about the age of your son here, and she'd have a whole herd if I let her."

Rebecca took the proffered brush and glanced down to see Jonah shaking out his hand. "You okay?"

His quick nod as he returned to his vigorous brushing told her he hadn't planned on her seeing him.

"Brushing is hard work if your arms aren't used to it." Mac stepped back and let her brush for a few strokes. "No, like this." He laid his hand over hers to put more pressure on the brush. The tingle that flew up her arm made her catch her breath.

"I—I see."

When he stepped back, her side felt the chill again. His body heat had shielded her, warmed her. She hadn't felt such comfort in a long time. If comfort was the proper word.

She grinned down at Jonah when she went around to his side of the horse, shaking out her arms like he had. His eyes danced as he nodded.

"That looks pretty good. Now I'll pick his hooves. You can see he isn't wearing shoes. . . ."

At Jonah's glance at his own sneakers, Mac chuckled. "You're right, Son. Cody's shoes are different than yours. See that?" He pointed at a metal arch on the post. "Those are Cody's shoes. They are nailed into his hooves. . . ."

Jonah took a step back, horror rounding his eyes and mouth.

Mac smiled again and shook his head. "No, it doesn't hurt him, any more than cutting your toenails does." Jonah nibbled on his bottom lip, his eyes still shadowed with doubt. "Here, I'll pick his hooves and show you."

Mac picked up one of Cody's front feet, dug the hoof pick out of his pocket, and pointed out the hoof wall, the tender frog, and the dirt that he dug out. "If Cody gets a rock in here by the frog, he could go lame and limp like if you had a rock in your shoe. If his hooves are never cleaned out, he could get an infection. I'll let you do this next time."

Rebecca sucked in a breath, loud enough that Mac looked her way. "What if. . . ?"

"Cody stepped on him or knocked him over?" He finished the sentence for her.

She nodded.

"That's why I'm teaching him the right way. Getting stepped on happens sometimes. You just learn to keep your feet out of the horse's way." His gentle voice calmed the up-speed of her heart. She'd not thought of all of this when she agreed to bring her son to befriend the horse. But one look at Jonah's face told her they were doing the right thing.

A brief nod said she—she what? Agreed? Approved? What?

The phone on the tack wall rang.

"Excuse me." Mac left them with the horse and Jonah picked the soft brush out of the bucket and, tugging Cody's head down to his level, began brushing the horse's face. Cody's eyes closed again, and he slightly leaned into the brush.

"He likes that."

Jonah nodded. He did, too.

Mac returned. "I'm really sorry, but I'm going to have to go deal with that guy. He owns the house I'm working on and can't get out there during the week. We won't get to the riding today after all." He squatted down to Jonah's level. "Next time, all right?"

Rebecca could feel relief soothe her neck and shoulders.

Jonah nodded and dumped his brush in the bucket. He turned and stroked Cody's nose, leaning his forehead against the horse's face. The sweet vision of the two caught her heart. She glanced up in time to see Mac smile and nod. He laid a hand on her son's shoulder, his other on the horse's neck.

"You did good, Jonah. Real good." He turned to look at Rebecca. "Could you come back tomorrow afternoon? I get home from church about twelve-thirty or so."

Thoughts of the amount of work she had left to do made her pause.

"If you want to, that is."

Jonah left the horse and came to stand by her side,

taking her hand and imploring her with every ounce of his being.

"If you're sure it's no bother. I mean. . ."

"I don't ever say something I don't mean."

At the firmness in his voice, she nodded. "We'll see you then."

As the three of them walked on up toward the house, she noticed Jonah slip his other hand into Mac's. Was this whole thing going too fast? Fear bombarded her. What if Jonah got hurt? What if. . .he fell off? What if the horse. . . ?

Ah, but what about you? The little voice made her grit her teeth.

five

"Is that all you wanted?"

Mr. Miller took a step back. "Ah yes, I mostly wanted to touch base with you, check on that addition. Sorry if I took you away from something important, but this is the only time I have for the next two weeks."

Lord, save me from overzealous home owners. Mac accepted his apology with a shrug. "I'm here now, so let me show you what I had to do. I wrote up a change order with the extra charge on it. I have a copy for you and one for Jim in the truck." After pointing out a problem they'd not anticipated with the addition and listening to the man compliment him on a fine job so far, Mac handed him the change order, shook hands, and watched as the man climbed back in his SUV and wheeled out the drive.

Baby-sitting owners wasn't on his list of pleasurable

duties, but sometimes that came with the territory. Since he had yet to overcharge or cheat anyone, he had to remind himself that all plumbers and plumbing contractors didn't work by his standards. Keeping on top of the project was wise for someone having a house built. It helped, however, if they had some kind of rudimentary knowledge of construction.

Or trusted their contractor. Jim Benson was no more in the business to cheat someone than he was. Otherwise he wouldn't work with him.

So, I'll see them again tomorrow. Instead of turning on Banducci Road and going west toward his place, he turned right and headed to town. If he put a roast in the oven, surely they would stay for dinner. After buying more than just a roast at the supermarket, he loaded the six grocery bags in the rear seat of his king cab and headed on home. Good thing the housecleaner had come this past week.

That evening, he kept one eye on the football game and one on the phone. Should he call her and apologize for running off like that? And invite them to stay for dinner? What if they already had other plans? But she'd said they didn't know very many people. "Good grief, Turner James McNeally, you are dithering like a teenager asking for a date. What's come over you?"

Bungee rose from his place on the rug by the wood-burning stove and came to lay his head on Mac's thigh. His brush of a tail wagged, and Mac could swear his eyebrows rose in question.

"No, it's not your problem, Boy." He thumped the dog's sides and rubbed his ears, gaining a whimper of pleasure for his efforts.

The Sunday school class he taught on *The Letters of John* seemed to last twice as long as the allotted hour, and the pastor doubled his sermon time, or at least it felt that way. Mac was headed out the door without staying for coffee when one of the men stopped him.

"Hey, what's your hurry?"

"I have a boy coming to ride Cody, my daughter's horse."

"That was your ad in the paper then?"

"Yep. And it worked. Nice little boy." *With a nice mother.*

"Well, good for you. I thought that was your number. Told Maggie, 'See, Mac's making changes.' "

"Well, I don't know about changes but. . ."

The man thumped him on the shoulder. " 'Bout time's all I can say."

"See you." Mac scuttled out the door before anyone else could grab him. He knew this was totally unlike his normal behavior, but so be it. Halfway home, the man's words came back to him. *About time for what? Company for Sunday dinner?* He and Dani frequently had company. He was known as a pretty good cook in general and of gourmet-chef caliber on the barbecue. The youth group used his pool, as did other groups from the church. His home was always open.

Except for today. Today it was open to someone different.

He dumped a packet of onion soup mix on the roast and, after wrapping it in aluminum foil, set it in a pan and put the pan in a 300-degree oven. After all, Jonah might like to ride for quite awhile, at least by the time he groomed Cody again. And the longer the roast cooked, the better it would taste. He peeled potatoes and left them soaking in a pot of water. Glancing at the clock, he realized he had a choice—make the salad or go groom Cody himself. What was best for the boy? For Cody? After all, that's who this was all about. A needy boy and a lonely horse.

Let alone a lonely man. The thought brought him to a halt, staring out the window. Was he lonely for a woman? Or would anyone do? Friends and family had been fine up to now. What was different?

He closed his eyes. Rebecca appeared on the backs of

his eyelids. Just as he had seen her in a dream. One he'd forgotten about until just now. So why was he attracted to her?

Lord, help me out here. Did You bring her to the ranch for a reason? Is this some part of Your divine plan? You know, I've told You all along that when You have the right woman for me, You have to bring her into my life. I'm not going searching. I tried that. Never again. He shuddered at the memory. One of the women from church had said she had a sister she wanted him to meet. He'd gone along with the plan. Dated her a few times. But, when she began to want more than friendship, he realized he wasn't ready for that. And she wasn't the right one. Clingy had never set well with him. Most likely because he'd been married to a strong woman, and they'd grown into the kind of marriage that people envied.

Not that it had started out that way.

Bungee's barking tore him from his reverie as a familiar SUV drove in and parked by the gate to the yard. Jonah bailed out and allowed the dancing dog to lick clean his ears, cheeks, and every other part of his face that Bungee could reach.

Mac snagged his sheepskin vest off the hook and shrugged it on as he exited through the door. The laughter and barking hit him like a pillow in the face.

If only. . . He sucked in a deep breath and clamped a hand against the door frame to keep himself from reeling backward.

His son used to play like that. Dani had played like that, too. The memories flipped through his mind like a movie on fast-forward. Or, as in this case, in reverse.

"Are you all right?" Rebecca stood at the bottom of the three stairs leading up to the porch.

"Ah, yes." Mac blinked and swallowed. He shook his head, ever so slightly, to clear it and took another breath. His solar plexus ached like he'd been sucker-punched. "Just swallowed wrong, I guess." He could feel heat creeping up his neck. He pulled the door shut and forced a smile to his lips.

"We can come back another time."

"No, no, I've been looking forward to making up for running off like I did yesterday. In fact. . ." He could now breathe easily again, and the world had tilted back to where it belonged. He motioned to the house. "I was hoping the two of you could stay for dinner. I put a roast in earlier, so it won't take too long to finish fixing the meal." *You sound like a kid asking for a date and trying to hide your zits.*

"Ah, if you're sure that would be no bother. I mean, that wasn't in the ad."

Was she teasing him? Mac stopped on the step above her and searched her eyes. A glint? He nodded. "Nope, forgot to include that."

Jonah came to stand by his mother, his eyes dark and serious, the laughter gone.

"Well, Cody's waiting. I told him you were coming, and he got all excited."

Jonah looked at him out of the corner of his eye, his head tipped slightly forward. As if assessing Mac and finding him for real, he grinned and tugged on his mother's hand.

Mac tousled the boy's hair. *Ah, if only we could get you to talk. I know you must have all kinds of words you've been wanting to say.* "Let's stop by the tack room and get treats for you know who. Today I won't have any, so you can get his attention real easy." Mac looked toward the woman. "You want some, too?"

Rebecca shook her head. "No, let's keep this all for Jonah."

Wise woman. Over the boy's head, Mac smiled his approval. He lifted the lid on the barrel that held the horse cookies. "Put some in your pockets, too."

Jonah gave him a questioning glance but did as told.

"Can you whistle?" Mac used the three-tone whistle he'd used before to call Cody.

53

Jonah shook his head, his lips curving down.

"Well, perhaps one day. Some things you have to practice."

When they reached the fence, Mac whistled, and Cody raised his head. When Mac whistled again, the horse broke into a jog, then a lope.

"Did you train him to come like that?" Rebecca stood behind her son, hands on his shoulders.

"No, Dani did. Horses learn real quick if food is involved, and she always had treats for him. She used to raid the carrot rows in the garden on her way to the pasture. Sometimes she walked on out to get him and ride back, no bridle, halter, or anything. He's been both leg and voice trained. The two were a real joy to watch in the show ring."

Cody trotted right up to the fence and hung his head over the rail. His ears pricked toward Mac, but when Jonah palmed a treat, he took it immediately. Jonah flashed his mother a cheek-splitting grin. Cody crunched happily, keeping his gaze on the boy.

"Go ahead, pet him."

Jonah took a step closer and rubbed between Cody's eyes, then when the horse lowered his head more, up around the ears. Cody nosed Jonah's pocket with a gentle nudge. The boy shot a glance at the man for approval and, at Mac's nod, dug another treat out of his pocket.

"Come on, Old Horse, let's get you brushed so you can earn your keep and give this boy here a ride." Mac turned at the sound of a quick breath. "He'll be fine, Rebecca. You don't have to worry."

The grooming went just like the day before, only this time Mac stood back and let mother and son do all the dirty work, except for picking the hooves.

"I'll let you do this next time, so watch carefully. See how I lift his hoof and rest it on my knee or between my knees? That way you can use both hands, like farriers do." Jonah's eyes lit in question, so Mac continued. "A farrier is a person who shoes horses. When my daughter comes home from school next spring, we'll put shoes back on Cody so Dani can ride him up in the mountains. Here in the pasture he really doesn't need them. I trim them up once in awhile. See, horse's hooves keep on growing like your toenails do." By the time he finished his explanation, the hooves were clean, and he'd gone to the tack room for the saddle.

"Watch how I put the bridle on and saddle up. Next time will be your turn." Mac laid the Indian-patterned blanket on Cody's back and swung the Western saddle into position. By the time he'd tightened the girth and adjusted the length of the stirrups, he'd given them a full rundown on the process.

"You explain things well." Rebecca stood at Cody's head and rubbed his ears while Jonah stroked his neck.

"Been at it a long time."

"You had horses as a boy?"

"Yep, we had a ranch then, too. My father stills runs it up in Walker Basin. In the mountains north of here." He answered the question he saw coming before she could ask it.

Unhooking the halter, he slid it to Cody's neck. "If you do this, your horse isn't free to run while you put the bridle on. Just a safety measure and a good habit, though Cody wouldn't try to get away. Now you hold the bridle like this and slide the bit between his teeth."

"What if he. . ."

"Cody won't bite. He's too well trained, but when you hold it right, you can't get bitten anyway. Then you slide his ears through the headstall and buckle the chin strap." Mac did each of the actions as he talked about them, flipping the reins up around Cody's neck to cross at his withers. "Now we'll lead him outside, and I'll show you how to mount. Oh, wait a minute. I forgot." He headed for the tack room and returned with a helmet. "Here." He set it on Jonah's head. "It's a bike helmet, but it works." He watched while Jonah buckled the strap. "Good."

Jonah hung back by his mother as they all walked out of the barn to stand in the sunshine.

Mac looked down at the boy. "Guess I'm going to have to build a mounting block again. Your legs are so short." He looked around to see a black heavy plastic feed tub just inside the barn door. "Go get that." He pointed. "The tub will work fine."

Jonah handed it to him, and Mac set it upside down and patted the base. "Now you step up on here, and you'll be able to get your foot in the stirrup. Hope I got them the right length, but we can adjust that."

Jonah looked up at his mother, over to Mac, and back at the black tub. He took in a deep breath and let it out, straightened his shoulders, and climbed upon the tub. He patted Cody's shoulder and stared at the saddle.

"Okay, now you are going to hang onto these leather strings, called latigos, and put your left foot in the stirrup. I'll give you a boost up this time. You'll straighten your left leg and swing your right leg over the saddle. Understand?"

Jonah's nod could not be mistaken for excitement by any stretch of the imagination.

"You want me to hold Cody still?" Rebecca asked.

"If that would make you feel better. He's been trained to stand still for mounting."

Rebecca moved to the horse's head and looked for something to hold onto.

"Take his reins gently under his chin." Mac glanced over his shoulder. "Don't worry, he isn't going to bite." He watched as she gingerly grasped the reins. *Good grief.* "Okay, Son, let's get you mounted up. Grab the latigos, foot in the stirrup."

Jonah did as he was told until he tried to get his foot into the wooden stirrup. When he started to lose his balance, he looked to Mac.

"Be careful," his mother said, taking a step forward.

Mac gave her a look that made her clench her teeth.

"Okay, let me help you this time." He helped put the boy's foot in the stirrup, all the while bracing him with the other arm, then lifted so Jonah found himself in the saddle. The boy's grin said it was all worth it. "That'a boy, just takes some doing the first time out. I can see for sure I need to get a mounting block built again. Why sometime even your mother might want to ride."

Her shudder at his words made him smile inside. But what if she never learned to care about horses and riding? His smile dissolved.

*F*at chance," Rebecca muttered under her breath.

Cody shifted his front feet, and Jonah clutched the saddle horn with both hands.

"That's good." Mac patted the boy's knee. "Looks to me like these stirrups fit pretty well. Stand now, so we can make sure." At Jonah's look of panic, Mac shook his head. "Nothing to worry about, just rise up on the balls of your feet in the stirrups. Cody isn't going anywhere."

"He—he's so high up." Rebecca tried to smile at her son, but her cheeks and mouth froze with the effort.

"He's fine, aren't you, Jonah? Solid in the saddle. Good, now stand."

Jonah did as he was told and, when nothing scary happened, he grinned at his coach and sat back down.

"Good. You want a bit of air between you and the

saddle seat. Now I'm going to lead you around so you can get your balance. Do you ride a bike?"

Jonah nodded, his smile telling how he loved his bike.

"He learned to ride that really quickly. Took off the training wheels within weeks." Rebecca's smile came more easily this time. She nodded to Jonah, who smiled back at her. *He looks more comfortable with this than I am. This horse is just so big. And that gives him so far to fall.* Cody nudged her, and she took a step backward. "Easy, Horse."

"His name is Cody." Mac's voice wore a slightly flat tone that Rebecca picked up on as remonstrance.

Well, what do you want from me? I never claimed to know anything about horses.

"Okay, Jonah, are you ready? We'll go slow."

Jonah nodded, and Mac took the reins from Rebecca. "Maybe you'd like to wait over by the car?"

"I guess." *Feels like you want me out of the way. I can't help it if I am a worrier. You would be, too, if this was your only son on the back of a huge horse for the first time.* She stepped back, and Mac walked forward, slowly as he promised. She looked up at Jonah's face and almost pulled him off the animal. His eyes were wide open, his teeth clenched, leaving his mouth in a grimace—of what? Fear, no, terror? He clung to the saddle horn like a lifeline about to be jerked out of his grasp. This was not a good idea, not at all.

"Good, Jonah. You're doing great."

No, he's not. Can't you see how frightened he is? She took a step forward, but the look Mac sent her locked her in place. She felt a cold nose in the palm of her hand and looked down to see Bungee sitting at her feet, his strange eyes imploring her attention. He wagged his brush of a tail and whimpered deep in his throat. She patted his head, then turned to watch her son.

Mac turned Cody in an easy arc and headed back toward the car. He said something to Jonah that Rebecca couldn't hear, but the smile on her son's face said far more than words. Once the original trepidation passed, he was loving every minute of his ride. When he let go with one hand to lean forward and pat Cody's shoulder, his mother took a deep breath and sighed, puffing her lips in the motion.

"Good, Jonah, good job."

Jonah nodded hard enough to make his bangs flop, and his cheeks bracketed a heart-stopping grin.

"Okay, now, Jonah, I'm going to lead Cody around in a circle and then a figure eight so you can feel how his body moves." Mac accompanied his words with the appropriate actions.

Rebecca watched them walk in figure eights and circles, saw her son's shoulders relax, watched him stand at Mac's instructions, sit back, and finally take both hands off the horn at the same time. "He's so brave." Bungee nosed her hand, drawing her attention back to him. "Go away, Dog, I need to watch my son."

Jonah waved to her when they drew closer again. Rebecca waved back, fighting eyes that wanted to water. "Lookin' good there, Sport."

When Mac stopped Cody by the overturned black tub, she wandered over to watch what they were doing.

"Now, hang onto the saddle horn and swing your right leg back over the cantle." Mac laid his hand on the rolled leather that formed the back of the seat. "And lower yourself until your right foot touches the tub, then take your left foot out of the stirrup and you are down. I'm right here to help you."

"You want me to hold Cody?"

"If you like, but he is ground-tied. When his reins are on the ground, he stands still."

Rebecca glanced from him to the horse and back.

"Yes, I'm sure."

She took the reins anyway, up under Cody's chin like Mac had shown her before.

"Okay, Son, you ready?"

Jonah nodded and leaned forward, swinging his right leg back and around. His hands gripped the saddle horn until his knuckles turned white. He hung there.

"Not to worry. I'm here for you." Mac clamped his hands around Jonah's waist. "Now, together. Lower yourself."

Rebecca watched, amazed at the patience of the man, not rushing Jonah, not going ahead of him, but letting him do the things in his time and learning all the while. *How often do I rush him, do something for him because he doesn't do it immediately?*

Jonah found the bucket with the toe of his shoe and looked up at his hands strangling the saddle horn. Slowly he let go with one and transferred it to the latigo dangling from a silver conch just to the back of the saddle seat. He slid his other hand over the pommel and caught that latigo, now able to set his right foot flat. With a whoosh of a sigh, he pulled his other foot from the stirrup and stood on both feet.

"Very good. That was very, very good." Mac laid a hand on the boy's shoulder and squeezed.

Jonah beamed at his mother and gave a slight shrug as if to say *no big deal.* He turned to Mac.

"You want to mount and dismount again? That would be a good thing for you to do."

Jonah nodded, turned, and grabbed the latigos. By the time he'd gone through the process four times and was standing back on the ground, Mac flipped the tub over and handed it to him. "You take that back where it belongs, and we'll put Cody in the pasture. You've done very well for a first-timer."

Mac looped the reins over his arm, and Cody followed beside him as if the two were out for an afternoon walk. "You coming?" he called over his shoulder when Rebecca walked toward the corral gate.

"You sure you want me along?" As soon as the words were out of her mouth, Rebecca felt the heat flame up her neck. What a thing to say. Where had her manners gone?

"Of course." The chuckle followed the words over his shoulder.

"Come on, Bungee, no sense both of us feeling left out." But at the barn door, she hung back as Mac instructed Cody how to remove the saddle and put the tack away. He handed the reins to Jonah, and the two walked to the back door that Mac slid open for them.

"Okay, now unbuckle the chin strap and pull the headstall over his ears. He'll drop the bit." Jonah did as told, his eyes wide as Cody opened his mouth to let the bit fall and then snuffled Jonah's hair before snorting. He nosed Jonah's jacket pocket and, after a quick check with Mac to see if it was all right, Jonah dug out a treat and palmed it for the horse. When Cody nosed for another, Jonah shook his head and raised both his hands, palm up. Cody sniffed them both, waited for Jonah to finish rubbing his face, and then walked off to stop a few paces out. He looked back around his shoulder as if he might have changed his mind, then shook all over and ambled off to the pasture.

Rebecca stared after the retreating horse, running the entire scene through her mind again. If she didn't know better, she would have thought that horse was talking with her son, in spite of neither of them being able to say a word. Were all horses this smart and intuitive, or was Cody something really special? Did she dare ask Mac? No, he would be prejudiced. After all, Cody was his horse, or rather his daughter's.

"Come on, let's go eat." Mac waved Jonah ahead of him, slid the door closed, and strode up to where she waited. "You hungry? I sure am."

"Yes, thank you. And thanks for your time here with Jonah. What a gift you are giving us."

"My pleasure." Mac put a hand under her elbow to turn her in the direction of the house and laid the other hand on Jonah's shoulder, familiar as if he'd been doing both motions forever.

Her elbow sent off sparks.

Mac slid open the glass door and motioned her ahead of him. "Make yourselves comfortable while I check on the dinner. Bathroom is down the hall, first door on your left."

"Is there anything I can help you with?" Rebecca glanced around the room, taking in the leather recliner, leather sofa, with an Indian rug of red and black designs on a cream background thrown across its back. A cowhide on the floor looked as if someone had divided the two red/burgundy sides with a strip of white that had also covered the belly and lower legs. Mounted long-horns, three feet between the tips, protected the field-stone fireplace. Definitely a man's room—a man who loved all things Western, including two framed, silvered boards, one on either side of the fireplace, with foot-long segments of old rusted barbed wire staggered down the length. Full bookshelves covered the remaining expanse of wall, drawing her attention as she followed Jonah down the hall to the bathroom. Such a comfort-able house. It reached out and wrapped its arms around them as if they'd been coming to visit for years.

"Use soap."

Jonah looked at her like she'd said too much, since he already had the bar in his hands.

"Sorry."

He nodded, washed, and dried his hands, then headed out the door and back down the hall.

Even the bathroom showed Mac's love of ranching things, with another set of horns, these much smaller for the towel rack, the mirror framed in aging silvered boards, and the toilet lid covered in part of another cowhide. A cartoon model of an old cowboy reclined on the top of the tank. Even the towels were brown.

Rebecca washed, checked her hair in the mirror, and replenished her lipstick. *Okay, now go out there and enjoy what's left of the afternoon. A good meal ahead, pleasant company.* Why was she hanging out in the bathroom? The question spurred her out the door without an answer.

She paused to watch Jonah setting the table. Mac arranged a mixture of lettuce leaves on plates while Bungee watched from a rug by the door. Feeling about as necessary as a toothache, she wandered to stand in front of the bookshelves, reading titles. Cattle veterinarian books, books on horses, Civil War tomes, Time/Life series on Indians, a wide range of fiction of all genres, biographies, children's books, and a set of encyclopedias. The well-polished trophies on one shelf all belonged to his daughter, Danielle. Family pictures took up some space, Mac and a smiling woman with two small children, the boy younger than the girl. A head shot of the woman, school pictures of the children, an eight-by-ten of Danielle on Cody, running full-out. All clean and dust free. The man either had a good housekeeper, or he was a neat freak. She wasn't sure which. The place was certainly not like other male domains she'd visited, not a hint of clutter, nor the look of decorator-done furnishings, just comfort—Western style.

She turned around to find Mac watching her, a half-smile brushing his mustache. "Can I get you something to drink? Coffee? Tea? Soda? I have a well with great water. . . ."

"Is the coffee made? I mean, I don't want you to go to a whole lot of trouble."

"Ready to pour. You take sugar or cream? She shook her head, so he glanced to Jonah, who was making sure the silverware lined up. "Jonah, what about you?"

"He'll have milk if you have it."

A slight frown tightened his forehead, and the look he gave her would take some deciphering, but he filled a coffee mug and held it out to her. She crossed the room and took it, cradling it in her hands.

"Thanks." She inhaled the flavor and smiled over the rim. "Smells wonderful. Is there anything I can help you with?"

"You can lean against that counter, enjoy your coffee, and watch me make gravy." He nodded to a cream-tiled countertop next to the sink.

"If that's all. . . " She did as he'd suggested, crossing her ankles and sipping. The man certainly made good coffee. "You grind the beans?"

"Earlier this morning. I was hoping you would stay."

"Your daughter won a lot of trophies."

"Yep. She and Cody were a real team, barrel-racing and trail-riding mostly. She won some in 4-H, too, fitting and showing, that kind of thing." At the questioning look she gave him, he grinned with a slight shrug. "I'll get out the picture albums after we eat and explain what those things are then. Pictures make it easier."

"I'd like that." So where was his wife, the boy? Looking around the great room, she saw no other evidence of a woman's touch other than the pictures. "Your son, how old is he now?"

Mac paused in stirring the rich brown gravy. "He's waiting for us in heaven. He and my wife were killed in a fog-related car pileup near Caliente, ten years ago in January." The words lay between them like a chasm that looked too wide for her to cross.

"I—I'm sorry." She studied his profile as he went back to stirring. "Bad enough losing a mate, but I can't imagine how bad it must be to lose a child." Her glance went to Jonah, now sitting on the rug by the door with Bungee draped over his crossed legs.

Mac nodded. "It was real bad. For a time there, if it hadn't been for Dani needing me, I wasn't sure if I'd live or die."

"What helped you?" The question seemed pulled from her.

"Jesus. My family. God's Word. I never spent much time with my Bible up till then." He poured the gravy into a gravy boat and handed it to her, nodding toward the table. "I thought God hated me or I had done something so terrible wrong that I didn't deserve to have a family." He followed her with a platter piled high with sliced roast beef surrounded by potatoes and carrots and set it in front of the place setting at the end of the table.

"Wh—what made you change?" She forced the question past lips that tried to stay glued to her teeth. *What kind of nerve do I have asking questions like these? Such bad manners.*

He stopped in front of her. "Time and the grace of Almighty God. In spite of what the songs say, a broken heart does heal."

His eyes held the wisdom of the ages, and warmth

flowed from him to wrap around her, comfortable like a fleece blanket.

She fought the tears that threatened to overflow and turned away with a sigh. "Time to wash your hands again, Jonah." At his look of amazement, she added, "You played with the dog."

He shrugged and headed for the bathroom.

Seated at the table a few minutes later, Mac bowed his head. "Let's say grace." He waited a moment. "Heavenly Father, thank You for this food and my new friends. Thank You for the time to enjoy each other. In Jesus' precious name, amen." He looked up and smiled at each of them. "Now, I hope you are really hungry. Pass me your plates since that platter is too big to pass."

They both did and he added slices of roast, then the vegetables, until Rebecca said stop. He handed Rebecca her plate, then Jonah.

"Here, hand me his so I can cut up his meat."

"You cut up his meat? He's eight years old." Mac stared at Rebecca. His eyebrows nearly met above eyes that flipped from warm to cool, like a switch had been thrown.

Back off, Buddy. He's my son and I do for him what I think best.

seven

Lady, you are going to ruin that boy.

Jonah waved good-bye before getting in the car. Rebecca stared straight ahead.

Get over it, McNeally. If she wants to baby him, that's her right. He's her son after all. Shame they left early. No, more than a shame—downright sad. Mac shrugged into his sheepskin vest and, whistling for Bungee, he headed out to the cow pasture. This time he'd walk it; he needed the exercise and he needed to pound on something. Dirt was good for that.

You shouldn't have said that.

I know. It just slipped out.

You are usually so careful about what you say.

I know it! I said it just slipped out.

You better call her and apologize.

For what?

You know for what.

"Good grief, Lord, is this You telling me all this or just my overactive imagination?"

Bungee leaped at his side, yipping his answer, whether he understood the question or not.

After checking the water trough, Mac counted the cows and watched to see if anything appeared unusual. All there and no obvious difficulties. He turned and headed back to the house, the dark empty house that, if he'd kept his mouth shut, might still have the warm presence of an interesting woman and her just-as-interesting son.

He glanced at his watch and picked up the pace. Perhaps Dani would call tonight. Two hours' difference, seven o'clock there. He took the steps to the deck two at a time and pulled off his boots at the jack. Time for slippers, a cup of coffee, his chair, and the Sunday paper. Perhaps there would be a good movie on tonight. If not, he had a stack of books to be read, with a good suspense on top.

The phone rang just as he poured his coffee.

"Hi, Dad."

"Hey, Dani, I was hoping you'd call."

"Not sinking into loneliness, are you?"

"No, in fact I had company for dinner, Rebecca

Wilkinson and her son, Jonah. They answered that ad I told you about, so I'm helping Jonah and Cody get to be friends."

"And you invited them to dinner? Way cool. How does Cody like them?"

"Just fine. You know how he loves attention, but I think that horse reads people better than most psychologists. What's going on with you?"

"What did you mean about reading people?"

"Well, Jonah has a bit of a problem. He lost his daddy four years ago and hasn't spoken a word since."

"That poor little kid. What happened?"

"Military."

"Oh." A pause stretched before she continued. "I hope Cody can help him like he did me."

"Me, too." *If they ever come back. Me and my big mouth.* Mac shook his head and sighed. *But if she keeps on like she is, he will be ruined for life.*

"Dad?"

Her tone gave him the feeling he missed something she'd said. "Sorry, Honey, I got sidetracked for a minute. Did you ask me something?"

"Are you all right?"

Am I all right? Good question. "Sure I am." He hoped she didn't pick up on the effort it took to say those three little words. "So, back to my question, what's happening with you?"

"Well, I called to ask if you've reserved my tickets yet."

"Of course."

"Uh, would you mind if I came home a couple days later? I've been invited to go skiing in Colorado with Kelly. She's from there."

He started to say no, then changed his mind. "Yes, I mind, but if that is what you want to do, then you've surely earned a few days' break."

Mac knew Kelly was Danielle's roommate, and he also knew how much his daughter adored skiing. *But I miss you so; I want you to come home.*

"Oh, Dad, you are so good to me. We'd drive to Colorado, and I'd need to fly out of Vail. How about on the twenty-first?"

"Good as done. But I'm not decorating without you here, so don't expect the tree to be up and all that."

"Good, I want to help with the decorating anyway."

He waited while she told Kelly the good news and heard a squeal in the background. He rubbed a place on his chest, but it didn't go deep enough to heal the heartache. His baby was growing up, his only baby. The pain in his heart stabbed again, this time at the thought of a little boy who never had a chance to grow up and of a woman who, even though he knew resided in heaven, he still missed more than words could express.

Thoughts of Christmas always brought on the regrets, reminding him that, while he usually functioned just fine, sometimes the grief still hit him in the heart, and he was sure it cracked again. Without Dani here, it would most likely be even worse.

"Thanks, Dad, you're the best."

"You're welcome. Finals about on you?"

"Next week. Pray for me, okay? I still have a paper to finish before I can get ready for the tests."

She'd always been uptight before finals, and then she'd ace them. "I'm praying you'll be relaxed and give it your best."

"I miss you. You think sometime next semester, you could come visit me here?"

"We'll figure out a time."

"Thanks. Good night. Sweet dreams."

"You, too." He caught his lower lip between his teeth, the slight pain easing the burning on the backs of his eyes. "Bye." Her good-bye ringing in his ear, he laid the phone back in the cradle.

Okay, McNeally, cut the maudlin.

"Lord, take care of her. You know I can't. I put her in Your hands, but sometimes leaving her there is mighty hard. She's all I've got in this world that really counts." A picture of his mother and father flashed through his mind. "Well, you know what I mean." Next flashed a picture of Jonah on Cody with that heart-tugging grin of his.

Now, isn't that interesting? He leaned his head back against the cushion, replaying the afternoon. What a good time they'd been having up until Rebecca wanted to cut her son's meat. And he'd mouthed off. They'd stayed long enough to be polite, but she'd shut down faster than a camera click. *I suppose I do owe her an apology.* He waited, hoping God would say no. No such luck. Silence. Mac sighed.

Bungee rose from his place on the rug and came over to lay his chin on Mac's thigh, keeping a steady gaze on his face.

Mac stroked the dog's head and tried to think of ways around this new problem. He could ignore the incident and write them off, sure that Rebecca would never bring Jonah back out to the ranch again. He could call and see if she had warmed up any. He could call and apologize. He could go to bed and forget the entire thing happened.

"I could go apologize." The word *go* brought Bungee's front feet up in Mac's lap. He ruffled the dog's ear and pushed him down. "I'll call."

A whisper of air that sounded faintly like a chuckle tickled his ear.

The phone rang three times before she picked it up. In the meantime, he glanced at the clock to see it was already past nine. Where had the evening gone?

"Hello."

"Rebecca, this is Mac, and I'm calling to apologize for being such a critical host. How you raise your son is none of my business and I. . ." *Stop me anytime here.* "I just wanted to tell you that and ask you to forgive me." *And please don't take it out on Jonah and Cody that you are angry with me.*

"Oh. Ah, well. . ." The silence vibrated on the phone line. "I forgive you, I guess."

"Thank you." More silence. *Come on, McNeally, get your act together.* "And you'll bring Jonah out to ride?"

"Yes."

Was that a grudging tone he heard, or was he imagining things? "When?" He could hear pages fluttering.

"Is Tuesday all right?"

He groaned. "I have a meeting with the contractor at four. How about Wednesday?"

Again a pause. "That would be fine. Three-thirty or four?"

They settled on four and said their good-byes. Mac

hung up the phone and rehashed the conversation. So what kind of a woman was she? Did she hold grudges or would this be the end of it? She seemed a straightforward kind of person, but then what kind of judge was he? He'd only known two women really well in his life. His mother and his wife. Oh, three. Dani.

He scrubbed his hair back. "Come on, Lord, give me a break. What man alive is there who understands women, no matter how closely related they are?"

eight

"*He* apologized." Rebecca stared at the phone. "He actually called me and apologized." *And here I am talking to myself, which is happening more and more. I need a friend here in town. That phone bill last month was outrageous. And it was mostly to family.* Having parents stationed in Germany definitely helped support the phone company.

She ambled back to the master bedroom—half of which she'd turned into her office. In spite of not talking, Jonah was good company. However, the evenings stretched long and lonely after he went to bed. At least she always had work to do. She opened the file she'd been working with but couldn't bring herself to begin inputting data. Instead, she thought back to the disastrous dinner at the ranch.

The nerve of the man, telling her how to raise her son.

His tone, his words felt like she'd been whipped. Had he no empathy? After all, raising a child—a handicapped child, although she never used that word around Jonah or allowed anyone else to—was different from rearing other children. And so was being a single parent—er, mother, since he'd raised his daughter alone since she was ten.

The thought of losing both a child and a spouse at the same time set her stomach to churning. How ever had he made it through that? She was sure she would have bailed out on life. She had given it serious thought herself. If she hadn't had Jonah. . .

Lately it seemed her emotions were the ball in a Ping-Pong match.

Monday, when she picked Jonah up after school, he motioned her to drive out toward the ranch.

"No, we'll go out there on Wednesday. I talked with Mac. He didn't have time today or tomorrow."

Jonah clamped his arms over his chest and slumped in the seat, staring at the glove compartment, swinging one foot so that it banged the glove box.

"How was school?"

His lower lip came out, and he glared at her out of the corner of his eye.

"Jonah, it's not my fault. He has a business to run.

Remember?" Where had her normally cheerful child gone, and who was this grump in his place? "And stop kicking the dash."

Tuesday wasn't much better; and when Jonah woke up on Wednesday morning with a hacking cough and fever, she felt almost worse than he did.

"Sorry, Sport, no school today." She shook the thermometer back down and left the room to get the cough syrup from the medicine cabinet in the bathroom. A tear trickled down the side of Jonah's face.

"Are you sad about no school?"

He shook his head.

"About no Cody?" He nodded and let her gather him into her arms, sobbing and coughing against her chest. "Shhh, easy, you'll make yourself feel even worse. Here. . ." She mopped his face with a tissue and poured the cough syrup in the gauged plastic cup that came with it. "Drink this and sleep awhile and perhaps you'll feel better." At the hopeful look he gave her, she shook her head. "No, we won't be going out to the ranch today. I'll call and leave a message for Mac."

Jonah lay back against the pillow, his face pale enough that his eyes looked twice their normal size. Another tear meandered down his cheek, and he sniffed before turning over to clutch Jimmy Bear, a-fur-loved-off, one-eye-missing reprobate who had a tendency to get lost.

Rebecca leaned over and kissed Jonah's cheek before leaving the room. His sadness made her heart hang heavy in her chest. Here he'd found something he was so eager about and he couldn't go.

But you weren't going to let him go back out there anyway after the way Mac spoke to you.

But he apologized.

She ignored the accusing inner voices and dialed the phone. How she ever would have made the edict stick was beyond her. How could she even have thought of disappointing Jonah so?

You have to admit, you were looking forward to going back out there until. . .

Just shut up and leave me alone.

She snatched up the phone and punched in the numbers. At the command to leave a message after the beep, she did as she'd been told, then hung up.

This was definitely turning into a lousy day.

She spent the afternoon wrapping Christmas presents so she could get them in the mail. Only ten shopping days until Christmas, the television reminded her. With the shipping boxes all addressed, she took out the carton of house decorations and set out the nativity scene her grandmother had left her; candles with cheery rings; a soft sculpture snowman to sit outside by the front door; a grapevine wreath with tiny wrapped gifts, balls, and picks of holly and evergreens decorating the door. She set the artificial tree up in the corner but waited for Jonah to help decorate that.

With some Christmas music on the stereo, she placed the electric candles in the windows—something she'd learned when her family lived on a base near Washington, D.C. She'd been enthralled with driving through the towns and seeing all the candles in the windows. She had promised herself way back then that when she had a home of her own, there would always be candles in the windows. What a shame it had taken her until now to get them out this year. Such was the life of moving from place to place.

When the phone rang, she lifted the receiver and sat down in the recliner to talk.

Mac's voice made her sit a bit straighter.

"Cody is sure sorry Jonah couldn't come out and play."

"So is Jonah, although he's slept most of the day. He doesn't cry very often, but the tears were there. Made me feel like the Grinch who stole Christmas." She nestled the phone against her shoulder.

"Poor kid. There should be a law against getting sick before or during Christmas."

"I'd vote for it."

"Hey, I might have a surprise for him. Could you tell me your apartment number?"

"Two twenty-one, why?"

"Give me a few minutes and you'll know."

All she heard was the click and the dial tone. *What can he be up to?* She picked up the now-empty boxes and hauled them back to the storage area off their deck. Then, taking a string of lights, she wound them around the railing. Eyeing the deck above theirs, she saw the hooks someone else had inserted in the wood. The icicle lights would work there.

When she went back in the house, she found Jonah looking for her. The way he clutched her waist indicated his growing panic when he didn't find her.

"I'm sorry, Sport. I was just outside hanging up the lights. You go sit on the couch with the afghan, and I'll put the rest up so you can turn them on, okay?"

He shook his head and clung harder.

"You want some juice or hot chocolate?"

His nod set his hair to tickling her neck.

"Okay, juice?"

Head shake.

"Hot chocolate it is."

She set him on the counter, poured water in the tea

kettle, and set it on the burner. "Marshmallows?" Another nod. Taking out two packets of hot chocolate mix, she set them on the counter and paused at the ringing of the doorbell.

"Who do you suppose that is?"

Jonah shrugged and wiped his hand under his red nose. "Here's a tissue, Sport. Use it."

She went to open the door and stepped back in surprise. "Mac."

"I brought someone to cheer Jonah up." He whistled, and Bungee took the steps at a dead run to skid into the doorway. "Can he come in?"

"I–I suppose so." She ushered them into the living room. "Jonah, you have company." She heard him jump to the floor and come around the kitchen wall. A grin brightened his red eyes as the dog wriggled from nose to paws and everything in between. Bungee's tongue made lightning licks across Jonah's cheeks. His whimpers and yips made both the adults smile.

"Thanks, Mac. What a nice thing to do."

"You're welcome. You want Jonah and dog on the couch or in bed."

"Bungee on the bed?"

"Not unless Jonah invites him. Poor kid looks so miserable."

"I'm making hot chocolate. You want some?" The kettle took up singing just as she mentioned it.

"Sure."

"Marshmallows?"

"Of course."

She glanced over her shoulder to see Jonah lying on the couch with Bungee stretched out beside him, his tail wiggling half his body. Her son wore a smile that belied the red nose and smudged eyes.

She couldn't quit smiling herself. Mac came to cheer her son, actually the both of them, if she were honest. . . if the warm puddle in her middle were any indication.

It was a shame she hadn't baked cookies like she'd thought of earlier. Here it was almost Christmas and she had no baking done, but at least a good part of the decorating was finished and the boxes were ready to mail. She had made progress. She took a tray down from the top of the refrigerator and placed the three full mugs on it, adding napkins along with spoons for stirring.

Mac leaned against the sofa from his place on the floor in front of Jonah, who was lying on his side, head propped on his hand. The other hand stroked Bungee, who wore a blissful look on his mottled face.

"I didn't know dogs could look blissful," she said as she sat the tray on the coffee table.

"Of course they can. You just have to learn to read their body language. Bungee is especially adept at letting his feelings be known." Mac stroked his dog and got a clean ear in the bargain. "Aren't you, Fella?" The tail flipped into overdrive.

"Jonah, you better sit up to drink this."

"Bungee, down."

The dog paused, as if making sure the command was going to be enforced, then leaped to the floor to lay down with his chin on Mac's knee.

At the look on Rebecca's face, Mac smiled. "What can I say? The dog loves people."

"Is this a case of love me, love my dog?" *Oh my goodness, what did I say? What is he going to think? Rebecca, think before you speak.* She could feel the heat working its way up her neck.

The look in his eyes made her stomach curl up and purr.

"You could say that." His voice slowed and deepened, like the richest hot fudge sauce, sliding down the sides of a dome of French vanilla ice cream.

The thought of curling up in the circle of his arm flashed across her mind and brought on another wave of heat.

He lifted his hot chocolate mug to his lips and

sipped, then licked the marshmallow off his upper lip with his tongue. A bit of fluff clung to his mustache.

She took a swallow of her own—anything to keep her hands busy so her finger didn't sneak over there on its own accord and wipe that smidgen of sweet off and. . .

She got to her feet in one smooth motion but felt like a shuddering volcano inside. *Please, phone ring, someone, something, do something.*

"Can I get you anything else?" She could hear the shaking in her voice.

He patted the carpet beside him.

"Sit down and relax."

She sat in the chair at the opposite end of the room, as far away from him as she could get, and curled her legs beneath her.

This wasn't the way she had planned on spending her evening at all. Not in her wildest dreams.

But, oh my, it felt good.

He carried the sleeping Jonah back to his bed, then shrugged into his down jacket. "Thank you for a most pleasant evening. You make great hot chocolate."

"I forgot to even ask if you'd had dinner."

"I ate before I came. Rebecca, you worry too much."

"Occupational hazard, I guess, or maybe it's genetic. My mother worried and now I do."

"I see." He leaned against the door jamb. "Call me as soon as Jonah is better so he can come ride?"

"I will. Thank you." Her heart had picked up the beat as she continued to look in his eyes.

The urge to lean into his embrace surprised her so, she took a step backward, the magic spell tinkling in crystal shards at her feet.

Bungee licked her fingertips. Mac settled his dark brown Western hat on his head.

"See you soon." One finger burned her chin, then he and the dog went bounding down the steps, his boots ringing on the metal treads.

n i n e

$\mathcal{T}$hey're coming tomorrow, Cody," Mac said, dumping sweet molasses-smelling grain in the rubber tub.

The horse sniffed Mac's pocket before dropping his head to eat out of the tub. The sound of crunching filled the silence of the barn.

"How come you went and got so dirty?" Mac retrieved the brush and curry comb and set to cleaning up the mud-caked horse. "Just because we got rain, did you have to roll in every puddle?"

Cody's ears flicked back and forth, picking up every sound and nuance, as he nosed for the last few kernels.

"Now you stay clean tonight, or I promise you, you'll have to start spending the nights in your stall in the barn." Actually that was more a threat to himself, for someone had to clean out the stall, and he'd yet to train the horse or dog to do the deed. Or Jonah. How would Rebecca react if he said the boy had to shovel straw and manure out of the horse stall? All part of owning a horse, but then Jonah didn't own Cody. He just came out to ride and spend time with him.

That evening Mac picked up the phone and dialed the number he'd memorized while staring at it so long the night before. *Long* meaning the time it took to build up his courage to dial it. She had excellent phone skills, her voice warm and friendly from the first hello.

Had her voice warmed even more during their conversation? He promised himself to listen for that tonight.

"Hello?" Yes, nice and warm.

"This is Mac, just calling to check on the little guy."

"He's better. When I threatened to take him to the doctor, he started to get better. I think you have to scare the germs away at times."

Mac chuckled. "I can remember being sick. My mom would drive clear down to Bakersfield to the doctor. He'd say, 'How are you, Mac?' and I'd say, 'Fine.' I think she wanted to bust me one a few times."

It was her turn to chuckle. "I figure the worst must be over. He's wanting real food, not just Jell-O and Popsicles."

"Kids bounce right back as soon as the temp goes

THE GIFT

away, at least that was our observation. Good thing I don't get sick often."

"Me, neither." A pause lengthened.

"Did you get the rest of your lights up?"

"Yup, and the boxes mailed. My neighbor came in and stayed with Jonah while I ran errands."

Half an hour later they hung up, and Mac wasn't even sure where the time had gone. But she'd made him laugh, and he'd made her chuckle. He couldn't wait until the next day. He leaned back in his chair and stared into the flames dancing in the fireplace. She'd traveled the world over and he'd only seen the lower western states. She could speak three languages and he had only a smattering of Spanish to add to his English. She had no place to call home and he had a hunk of heaven right here in this lovely mountain bowl. A fair trade, all taken into account.

When the SUV drove in the next afternoon, Bungee lived up to his name, bouncing and leaping as Jonah jumped to the ground.

"Hey, Jonah, glad you got over that cold. Cody's been missing you."

Jonah smiled and, with an extra-wide grin, pointed to Bungee.

93

"Yeah, he missed you, too, but at least he got to go visit. On the way home, he told me he sure felt sad that you were sick."

Jonah raised his eyebrows and looked to his mother.

"You're right, Sport. He's pulling your leg." Rebecca flashed Mac a smile that smote him in the chest like being hit with a chunk of concrete.

When he could talk, he nodded at her. "You sure look nice in that scarf. Blue becomes you."

"Thanks, thought I might need something around my ears the way that wind is blowing. About the time I'm surprised to think we are being blown away, I remember the windmills and remind myself that white regiment on the east hills should have been a high wind warning when we moved here."

Mac pulled his wide-brimmed hat down more tightly. "Two more days and Danielle will be home. I can't wait for you to meet her." He led the way to the barn. "She said she hopes you love Cody like she always has. She's afraid he's grown lazy while she's been gone. Don't tell her, but he has." Mac lifted the lid on the horse-cookie bin, and Jonah put several in his pockets, then kept one in each hand. Mac whistled and Cody came jogging toward them; but this time, instead of going to Mac, he headed straight for Jonah, his nostrils fluttering in a soundless nicker.

"Hey, look at that, he's talking to you."

Jonah's eyes shone like he'd been given a gold medal. He palmed the horse cookie and Cody chewed it down and nosed for another, lipping it off Jonah's palm with a brushy upper lip. When Jonah headed for the barn, Cody walked right beside him, as if he had a rope around his neck.

"Will you look at that?" Mac shook his head.

"What if Cody steps on him?" Rebecca shoved her hands in her pockets as if to keep them from reaching for her son.

"Cody is careful about where he plants his feet, most of the time. And Jonah needs to watch out, too, but look at the trust growing there. Would you rather Jonah stayed with you and looked on rather than getting out there and experiencing everything he can?"

"Yes and no."

"Yes and no?"

"Yes, I want him to enjoy things. No, I don't want him hurt."

"None of us want those we love to get hurt, but sometimes you have to let loose enough for them to fly."

He watched her grit her teeth and take in a deep breath.

"He's so little."

"Maybe in size, but not in heart and that's what counts. You've done a good job with him, Rebecca, but you have to let him grow stronger, too."

She shot him a look that warned he was close to overstepping with his advice again, then she headed for the barn herself.

Jonah had Cody tied to the post, halter on correctly with the knot like the one he'd seen Mac tie. Brushes in hand, he'd begun the grooming, looking up to give his mother a grin and tilting his head in question to Mac.

"You did real well, Son, even to the knot. You are one observant young man, you know that?"

Jonah nodded and kept on brushing.

Mac motioned for Rebecca to help her son. "Without a stool, he can't reach the top line and rump."

"So?" She stared at his arm. "I don't see a cast."

Mac blinked, then burst out in laughter. *Ah, I see things are changing. Thank You, Lord.* "How about a bargain? You take that side. I'll take this one, and the loser has to pick the hooves."

Rebecca raised her spread hands in front of her and backed away. "No, I don't think so. I'll brush, but you take care of the hoof, hooves. Whatever."

"What are we going to do, Jonah?"

Jonah grinned, handed his brush to his mother, and, leaning over the grooming bucket, dug out the hoof pick and handed it to Mac.

Rebecca snorted, then giggled, ducking behind Cody, but Mac could hear her laughter.

Jonah giggled a little boy giggle that tickled Mac's funny bone even more than the laughter of the woman hiding behind the horse.

He chuckled along with them, bent to pick up a hoof, and proceeded to clean Cody's feet.

Once they'd saddled Cody, Jonah led the horse out into the corral. Mac walked beside them with a long coiled rope over his shoulder.

"This is a lunge line, and I'm going to snap it to the halter. That's why I left it on under the bridle. We'll begin with me walking beside you, and then as you get more comfortable, I'll let the line out. Okay?"

When they stopped in the middle of the corral, he motioned for Rebecca to put the black tub she'd been carrying down for a mounting block.

Jonah mounted, dismounted, and mounted again several times before Mac led him around the corral, first in circles, then reverses, figure eights, and more circles.

"You're doing a real good job there, Jonah. How does it feel?"

Jonah nodded along with a big grin and leaned forward to pat Cody's neck.

"If I didn't know better, I'd be thinking he's ridden for weeks instead of a few hours." Mac smiled at Rebecca, who'd gone over to lean against the rail fence.

"He's always picked things up quickly. Like his dad."

Was that pain he heard in her voice?

"Good. Okay, Jonah. I'm going to let this rope play out. Cody knows what he is doing, and now I want you to pick up the reins and hold them both in your right hand, together like this." Mac showed him how. "Good. Now your job is to keep the reins even. That's all you have to do and not pull back on them. If you pull back, Cody will stop. If you pull too hard, you will hurt his mouth. That's what the bit is for, to stop and guide him. You understand?"

Jonah nodded and strangled the reins.

"Easy, Son. Good riders have light hands."

Jonah relaxed his hand and received a nod of approval.

"Okay, Cody." Mac walked a few paces, then stopped and played out the lunge line so Cody walked farther away.

"Okay, Jonah. Gently pull back on the reins until Cody stops."

Cody halted, and Jonah's eyes widened to match his smile.

"Now, move your hand forward to signal him to move again."

They repeated the drill several times as Cody made his placid way around the corral.

"Keep your reins even. Good. Right there."

Mac tugged his hat farther down. About time to go in before they got blown off the earth.

Cody had walked to the end of the lunge line, at the far side of the corral, when a blue scarf fluttered across the open space.

Before Mac had time to react, Cody reared and leaped to the side to dodge the attacking missile.

Jonah sailed through the air and hit the ground in a belly flop.

ten

"Jonah! Oh my! Oh dear!" Rebecca catapulted into the solid wall of Mac's outflung arm. "Let me go!" *Get out of my way! Can't you see my son is hurt?*

"Leave him be, he'll be all right." *Please God, let it be so. That troublesome blue scarf. . .*

"What kind of inhumane monster are you?" She ripped at the arm holding her. "Let me go!"

"You go to the fence and let me tend to him."

"He's my son!" *He's choking and you won't let me through. I swear I'll sue you for every. . .*

"I know." His voice lost its edge of command and the softness melted her.

"You'll stay here?"

Her nod freed him to move toward the coughing boy,

who was already pushing himself to a sitting position. *Please Lord, let it be no worse than I think. I've been through this so many times before and she hasn't.*

Mac squatted by Jonah. "Easy, Son, you've just had the wind knocked out of you. You'll be okay in a minute or so."

Jonah coughed again and finally sucked in enough air to be reassuring. His red eyes took up half his face.

"Breathe easy, that's right."

Cody stood on the other side of Jonah, his nose nearly touching the boy's head. His ears pricked forward, and Mac would have sworn the horse had tears in his eyes.

"See, Cody is trying to apologize. He feels bad he was frightened, but it wasn't his fault; the scarf blew almost in his face. Horses get frightened like anyone else. He didn't mean to dump you like that."

Jonah looked up at the horse and wiped the dust from his eyes, eyes that leaked cleansing tears. He tried to shrug away, but Cody whuffled in his ear. Jonah couldn't help but smile and finally reached up and rubbed Cody's nose.

The horse sighed, as if in relief, and lowered his head even more.

"Do you hurt anywhere?" Mac kept a close watch to

see if Jonah flinched with any movement.

Jonah rubbed his chest.

"Good thing you had that heavy jacket and the helmet on, huh? They helped cushion you."

Jonah nodded and let Mac take his hand to pull him to his feet.

"That's the way. Feeling much better now?"

"Are you sure?" Rebecca stood right behind Mac. He hadn't heard her approach, he'd been so focused on Jonah.

Jonah looked at his mother and nodded again. He leaned into her when she put her arms around him, but when they started to walk away, Mac grabbed Jonah's arm.

"No, you don't. Time to get back up on Cody and finish your ride."

Matching looks of open-mouthed horror stared back at him. *Over my dead body, you monster. You want my son maimed for life?* She clung to Jonah's arm. "I think he's had enough for today."

Lord, give me strength. "You have to get back on now so you will always be able to keep riding." Mac kept his voice even and his gaze on Jonah, ignoring Rebecca. "Falls are part of the picture like sore shins if you play soccer. Come on, we'll lead him over to the tub."

All the while Mac spoke so gently, Jonah shook his head.

Rebecca shook her head, teeth gritted, and added a frown that would frighten Superman.

It didn't faze Mac.

"Jonah, get back up on the horse, now." His quiet steel brought Jonah's chin up and fire to Rebecca's eyes.

Jonah shook his head.

"Mac, no." Rebecca tried to kill him with her eyes. *He's not one of your cowboys; he's a frightened little boy.*

Dear God, make her give in. Help her realize her boy's future is at stake.

"Trust me, Rebecca, it's for the best." With one motion, he swept Jonah up in his arms and set him on the horse.

"Noooooooooo." Jonah's scream bounced off the barn walls and echoed across the valley. He choked the saddle horn with both hands, tears streaming down his face.

Dear God, he breathed. *Thank You, Jesus.* Mac glanced over his shoulder to see Rebecca's reaction, joy bursting like a geyser in his own heart.

"He—he—Jonah, you can talk." Instantaneous tears streaming, Rebecca started toward her son.

But Mac strongarmed her back to keep her from touching Jonah. "He has to do this," he hissed, hoping and praying she would give him even another two minutes.

"You masochistic monster. I swear if he is hurt, I'll kill you."

"I know, but he's not. Give him time."

All the while they argued, spitting words through clenched teeth, Mac kept his attention on Jonah as the rigidity left his back and he sat back in the saddle. His feet found the stirrups and finally he swallowed and looked to Mac.

"I hate you." Jonah's words came clearly and distinctly, each consonant and vowel like a tap against crystal.

Mac kept a smile from breaking his icy lips. "Be that as it may, you will ride now. I will lead you around the corral."

He talked; my son spoke actual words. Rebecca wrapped her arms around herself and watched as Jonah clutched the saddle horn again while Mac led Cody forward. *He spoke. He can talk.* The words drummed in her brain. *And I don't think he even realizes it. Mac does, though. I can see it in his face. But how could he be so insufferably cruel as to make Jonah get back up on Cody?*

But Jonah can talk again.

"Okay, Jonah, how are you doing?" Mac looked over his shoulder with a smile.

Although his eyes were still huge, the boy now rode easy in the saddle.

"I know you are mad at me, but someday you'll know that I did this for your best. By riding, you make Cody feel better, too. He tried to apologize back there, you know."

"I know."

Out of the corner of his eye, Mac saw Jonah lean forward and pat Cody's neck.

"You want to get off now?"

"Ye—n—ye—no."

"Was that a no?"

"Yes."

"So, yes, you want to keep riding, and no, you don't want to get off."

"Mr. McNeally!" The tone wore the patina of a child politely remonstrating with an adult.

Mac stopped and turned around to lay a hand on Jonah's leg. "You can call me Mac, Son. We're too good of friends for me to be Mr. McNeally. Okay?"

Jonah nodded and patted Cody again.

They circled the corral one more time before Mac had Jonah dismount.

Once on the ground again, Jonah threw both arms around Cody's neck when the horse lowered his head for a horse cookie. "Thank you, Cody." Cody whuffled

Jonah's hair and nosed at his pocket for another snack.

Rebecca, still casting daggers at Mac, shivered in the chill wind that had kicked up. *How can I thank a horse that might have killed my son? And the man who. . . ?*

How can you not. . . ? The voice overrode her arguments. She faced Mac.

"We are more grateful than I can say, Mr. McNeally. My son can talk." She blinked back tears. "Come, Jonah, we need to get going."

"All right." Jonah took the reins from Mac and led Cody back to the barn, shoved open the door, and led him inside.

The two adults followed without a word between them.

If I say one more word, I'll start to cry and never stop. She sniffed again.

Rebecca, how can I reach you? This should be a happy time. Let it go. Mac kept his arms at his side by sheer force of will.

Not much later, Mac waved them good-bye and sighed. *Why can't she be grateful her son is talking rather than being hung up on how it all came about?*

Sometimes it takes one tragedy to cure another; but this, while scary, wasn't a tragedy at all, but only a small bump in the road. Jonah was talking, and he wasn't afraid of the horse or riding. He'd made huge strides and all for the love of a horse.

His mother, on the other hand, was stuck in her fear and resentment. *Lord, at least she got her Christmas wish. Her son can talk again. And Cody had a friend for awhile. Perhaps they'll come again. We'll see.*

He shook his head. He sounded so philosophical and accepting, and yet his heart felt like someone had left open the barn door with a gale blowing in the dead of winter.

eleven

Rebecca Marie Wilkinson, you owe that man an apology!

"Hey, Mom?" Jonah, who had hardly stopped talking since they left the ranch those few hours before, called from the bathroom where he was playing in the tub.

Her son's call sent a thrill through her that zipped down to her toes and back to the top of her head, warming fingers and creasing her face in a smile without any effort on her part. *He can talk again, Jonah is talking.* She'd called her folks and Gordon's and, while Jonah was a bit shy, he had talked with them. Her mother-in-law had been crying when they hung up. So had she.

"Yes?" She ambled down the hall and leaned against the doorjamb. "What do you need?"

Jonah let bubbles drift down his arm. "When are we going back out to the ranch so I can see Cody?"

"You want to ride again?"

He nodded. "Cody needs me."

"I see." *How can I go out there without apologizing first? After all, it was my scarf that caused all the problems.* Guilt dug into her heart, ripping like a serrated dagger. *My scarf. My carelessness. If Jonah had been really injured, how would I ever forgive myself?*

"So when?" He looked up at her, his eyes full of questions. "Are you still mad at Mac?"

"Mr. McNeally."

Jonah shook his head. "No, he said I should call him Mac."

"When did he say that?"

"After I fell off. When we were walking around the corral."

"Oh." *So why didn't he tell me?*

Because you didn't give the man a chance to say two words. You hustled Jonah in the car and drove off as if you were fleeing an attempted murder. And the whole thing was your own fault.

She never had liked these inner arguments, especially when that little voice was right.

"Guess I can give him a call. Might have to wait until after Christmas now. He is probably pretty busy."

"Oh. But you'll call him?"

"Right now?"

"Yeah, now."

She tried. The line was busy. She heaved a sigh of relief.

Mac lay under the kitchen sink, the raised flooring cutting into his back. The aging pipes were not responding to a pipe wrench. His neighbor, Mrs. Fitch, who always said she was older than dirt, had called to report a stopped-up sink and, when first the plunger then the Drano didn't work, he'd gone out for the snake, only to find it not in his truck.

Confound that young pup, he thought. *What will it take to convince him to put things back?* So far orders, scoldings, and reprimands hadn't worked with his young helper. *Maybe I'll dock his pay; that ought to get his attention.* Of course before Randy had fallen in love, he'd been a good and dependable helper. But ever since he'd asked Lisa to marry him. . .nada.

Mac squirmed to get a better position.

"Can I help you?" The cigarette-scarred voice of his neighbor grated on his nerves—the three remaining nerves that screamed at him from the most-likely permanent crease in his back.

"No thanks, I'll have it in a minute."

"Okay, I'll be in the living room if you need me."

He leaned back and muttered. "When it's only me and the pipes, things go a lot smoother. Pipes are easier to fix than people any day of the week." Thoughts of a certain mother who had threatened to kill him for injuring her son flitted through his mind. And after all, the whole thing was her fault anyway. She was the one who wore the scarf that got loose and scared poor Cody half out of his wits. Poor horse, poor kid, poor. . .

He gave a mighty yank on the pipe wrench, and greasy, slimy water gushed out of the pipe and into his face. Thinking words that any good plumber uses with impunity, he bailed out from under the sink, wiping his face and wishing he were anywhere but there.

"I thought I would bring him in to see you, just so you could meet the real Jonah." Rebecca sat across from Amy Cartwright, the speech therapist. "He hasn't stopped talking since he started. It's wonderful."

"So tell me what happened."

Rebecca told her the entire story and leaned back in her chair. "Pretty amazing, wouldn't you say?"

Amy nodded, her smile lighting her eyes. "Leave it to Mac. That man has a heart big as Tehachapi Mountain."

"You know him?"

"Of course. He goes to my church. When you live in Tehachapi long enough, you get to know about everyone."

"Really?" More a statement than a question, Rebecca turned to look over her shoulder through the one-way window where Jonah played with a truck on the floor, making truck sounds as he drove the rig over a bridge he'd made of blocks. The bridge fell down and his laughter made his mother smile.

Along with the therapist.

"So what about you?"

Rebecca turned back. "Me?"

"Yes, I can see what a difference returning speech has made for Jonah, but what about you?"

Rebecca shrugged. "I'm happy and grateful and. . ."

"Now you have to let him grow up, you know. Let him do boy things and make decisions on his own."

"Are you saying I baby Jonah?" Her defenses rose like hackles on a dog. The thought of a man's shock at her cutting her son's meat zapped through her mind.

"Rebecca, I'm not accusing you. I really understand. When one has a child with a problem, our tendency is to try to make up for it, to make life easier."

Rebecca gripped her purse until her right forefinger ached, the one she'd once caught at the end with a softball. "I think it is time to go."

"I understand. But I do have your best interest at heart. Listen to him." They waited while Jonah brought the truck to a screeching halt, then smiled at each other.

"Thank you for your help." Rebecca rose and extended her hand.

"Ah, no." The therapist came around the desk and gave Rebecca a warm hug.

"Merry Christmas and what a wonderful present you received. Thank you for giving me one, too."

After an instant's hesitation, Rebecca hugged her back. "You are most welcome. Come on, Jonah. Get your coat." She waited while Jonah put on his coat and caught the smile in the therapist's gaze. "Merry Christmas indeed."

Once in the SUV, after he snapped his seat belt, Jonah turned to her. "Did you call Mac?"

Won't he ever let up? Rebecca shook her head. "Yes, but the line was busy." *No way I'll tell him I tried only once.* "I'll try again when we get home."

"There, what do you think?" Mac stepped back from placing the star on the top of the Christmas tree.

Danielle cocked her head and studied the decorations on the traditional pine tree in the corner of the great room. The white twinkle lights reflected in the huge window that overlooked the deck and Cummins Valley.

"We could have put more lights on."

"You always say that. We used all the strings and it took over an hour. I'd say we have enough."

"D–a–ad."

He slung an arm over her shoulders and drew her close to his side. "We didn't get a new ornament for this year." Since the children were little, every year they'd all gone shopping for a special ornament for the tree, one everyone had to agree on.

"I found us one in Vail. I'll go get it." Danielle ducked from under his arm and headed back for her bedroom.

She looks more like her mother every day, Mac thought, as he glanced at a picture of his wife on the mantle. *You'd be so proud of her.* Gleaming brown hair that swung straight from a center part, laughing hazel eyes, a pert, slightly turned-up nose, and a smile that could break a father's heart with its beauty.

The phone rang and, still thinking about his two girls, Mac answered.

"McNeally here."

"Mac, please don't say anything because I have to get this out while I still can. I'm sorry for the way I acted out in the corral, I'm sorry my scarf blew off like that, and

I'm sorry I never told you thank you for helping Jonah talk again." Rebecca sucked in a deep breath and let it all out to hear a gentle chuckle come over the line.

"Is that all?"

"Is there something else?" She heard the squeak on the last word.

"Not that I know of."

She sighed again. "Good. Now Jonah would like to come out and see Cody."

"Ah, good. When?"

"Would tomorrow be all right?"

"Could you stay for dinner? My daughter, Dani, is home from college, and I'd like you to meet her."

"Good. Four?"

"Three-thirty. Dani's been wanting to meet the young man who stole her horse's heart."

"Mac!"

"I'm teasing. See you then."

He hung up as Danielle came back in the room.

"Who was that?"

"Rebecca Wilkinson, Jonah's mother. They're coming out tomorrow."

"What time? I have a date, remember?"

"Oh, that's right. Well, you don't go till later, do you?"

She nodded and watched him, her face turned

slightly to the side. "Is there something going on here, other than a little boy and a horse?"

"Dani!" He paused and gave a half shrug. "We'll see?"

Danielle giggled and held up her ornament, a sway-backed Appaloosa horse on skis.

"Put it right in front. How funny." His chuckle made her smile.

"I hoped you'd like it."

"Dani, wake up, it snowed," Mac announced from the doorway of Danielle's bedroom the next morning. He glanced around the immaculate room, so different from the chaos of her growing-up years.

"Good, Dad, it's snowed in Chicago twice already and there was four feet of snow in Colorado." She pulled the last quilt her mother had finished up around her ears.

"But we might have a white Christmas here in Tehachapi."

Danielle rolled over and peered outside with one open eye. "Yup, it's snowing," she said and flopped back on the pillow.

Mac chuckled his way down the hall and went back to setting the ribs to boil so he could barbecue them for dinner. Bread was already rising in the bread maker, sending a yeasty fragrance through the house.

"That's not fair." Danielle, her slim body clad in gray sweats, her feet warm in fleece-lined leather slippers, ambled into the kitchen.

"What's not fair?"

"Fresh bread, that's what." She inhaled. "Oh man, that smells good. Is there any coffee?"

"Fresh pot." He nodded toward the coffee maker.

"What are you making?"

"Ribs for dinner."

"When I won't be here?"

"You are welcome to stay."

"But I promised Wendy."

"Your choice."

"Not fair." She took her coffee and sat on the field-stone hearth, the fire warming her back. "The tree is supremo."

"I know." He clicked on the stereo as he came by and strains of "What Child is This?" poured forth.

"The snow does look pretty." Danielle pointed to the two inches of white that capped the wooden railing around the deck. "Did you feed the birds?"

"Nope, left that for you to do." Mac put one foot up on the hearth and leaned on his knee, one hand holding the coffee mug. "Dani, I have a favor to ask."

"Shoot."

"Ah, when they come, will you take Jonah out to groom and tack up Cody? I need to talk to his mother."

"Ah." Her eyes danced.

"Now, don't go getting any ideas."

She assumed a most innocent expression. "Are you going to tell me you are 'friends. Just friends?' " One eyebrow arched.

"Get outta here, Brat." He swatted at her, but she ducked and left the room giggling. "Anything you say, Dad," floated back down the hall.

"Hey, Jonah, I hear you are quite the rider," Danielle said after they'd been introduced later in the day.

"I fell off."

"I've done that lots of times. Sure can hurt until you get your breath back, can't it?"

Jonah nodded. "But I rode again."

"So I heard. You always have to get back on so you don't go away afraid. My dad made me do that, too." She gave her dad a look filled with pure love.

"Uh-huh. Can we whistle for Cody?"

"Sure enough. Can you whistle?"

Jonah shook his head. "Can you?"

"Of course, come see." She reached for his hand and away they went.

"She'll be care. . ." Rebecca stopped and glanced at Mac before massaging her cheek with her tongue.

"Yes. Can I buy you a cup of coffee?" He motioned toward the house.

"Ah, this looks beautiful." Rebecca stopped just inside the sliding glass door to the great room and gazed at the tree. "It even smells real."

"The only kind. Have a seat."

She wandered over to the hearth and sat down. "I almost didn't come because of the snow, but then I decided that's what four-wheel drive is for, if I needed it."

"I'm glad." He handed her a coffee mug decorated with holly and berries and cupped his own in both hands. "You said you had something to ask me?"

"You know the other day?"

Which part of it? "Yes?"

"When you put Jonah back on the horse." She looked at him, half-hiding her face with the coffee mug.

"Rebecca. I couldn't treat Jonah any different than I would my own son. What more could I give him?"

"But what if he really had been hurt, not just the wind knocked out of him?"

"But he wasn't." *Here goes, Lord, give me the right words.* "Rebecca, you can't live your life in fear of what might have been." He watched her take a sip of the coffee and cradle the mug in both hands. "You have to give the people you love the chance to do the things they want in life, and trust God to take care of them."

"But *how* do you do that?"

"Every day, sometimes every minute when your mind insists on worrying, you have to put them back in God's hands and trust that He will take care of them because He said He would."

"But what if. . ." She smoothed a forefinger around the rim of the mug before looking back up at him. "What if you're not sure. . ." She licked her lips. ". . .Ah, if God really loves like that? I mean, I. . ."

"Would you let Jonah die to save someone else?"

She shook her head and glared at him. "Of course not."

"God did. He sent his Son to live and die here on Earth so that you and I might live forgiven and forever, and so we can trust Him to care for our children."

"You really believe that?"

"Yes." He leaned forward and looked into her eyes. "It is a gift, a gift you only have to open and then it is yours."

A tear brimmed over and meandered down her cheek. "In spite of all our losses?"

"He walks with us through our losses." He watched

questions float through her eyes like clouds blown before
a stiff wind. "I am more sure of this than of anything else
in my life."

"I–I want what you have."

"Dad, Rebecca, come see." Danielle called from the
open door.

"In a minute." *Lord, help her hear.*

"No, now. Come on."

Mac and Rebecca snagged their jackets off the chair
back as they headed out the door.

Down by the barn they brushed the snow off the
corral rails and leaned on the fence.

"Okay, Jonah."

Jonah led Cody up to the tub, mounted, and clucked
the horse forward. He rode Cody around the corral and
diagonal, along with turning and going the opposite
direction, then brought him to a stop in front of his
mother.

"Hey, Jonah, you did real well."

"Danielle said the snow would be a soft landing."
He grinned at the girl now leaning against the fence next
to her father. "If I fall off, I just have to get back on."

Rebecca glanced over at Mac, then up at her son. "I
guess that's right. You just have to get back on."

Mac leaned closer to whisper in her ear. "And you

just have to let go and let God take care of him."

Ignoring the warmth his breath caused, Rebecca scooped up a handful of snow and tossed it at him. "Easy for you to say."

twelve

ine and candle wax scented the air as Mac entered the church the next evening with Rebecca, Jonah, and Danielle. Christmas Eve always held a magical element for him: the flickering candles along the walls, the glittering tree near the altar, the hush of wonder as the organ played carols written long years before and now more meaningful than ever. Tonight, with the snow falling gently outside, the sanctuary seemed even more welcoming than usual.

He motioned, first, for Danielle to take their usual pew halfway up the aisle. He filed in behind her, followed by Rebecca and, finally, Jonah. Nodding and greeting those around, he sat down with delight bubbling behind his smile. Having Rebecca on one side and Danielle on the other made him want to give Jonah the thumbs-up sign, but the boy wouldn't understand. Or would he? Mac leaned around Rebecca, stuck both thumbs in the air, and received the same response, along with a smile that near to ruptured his heart.

"Thank you." His smile encompassed them both.

"For what?" Rebecca eyes widened slightly in question.

"For coming to church with us."

"You are most welcome, thank you for asking us."

How could such simple words carry such a chest-thumping impact? Their coming was one of his first and most important Christmas gifts. Other than Jonah's talking, of course. But then, that had been Rebecca's wish first. He'd just been privileged to be part of the process.

Rebecca bumped his arm taking her coat off and they exchanged smiles as he helped her. Way down inside, the desire to take her hand flared until he could think of nothing else. So he took it and squeezed gently, then stroked the soft skin on the back with his thumb.

Her sigh floated softly on the music.

"You all right?" He leaned close to whisper.

"Yes."

Danielle nudged him with her elbow, then winked at him when he looked her way.

Lord, how blessed I am. Thank You for these last weeks. I know Your love came down at Christmas, but I'm beginning to think—to feel that more love is growing right here. Is it possible we could become a family, is that Your purpose?

The heat from Mac's arm warmed Rebecca all over. One more thrill in a week of thrills. She listened to the music that seemed to carry her up so she could look down on the four of them, seated all prim and proper in the pew. What Mac had told her about trusting God made so much sense. All because she'd seen love in action. *If Mac could trust God after all that had gone on in his life,* she'd thought, *why not me?* So she'd dug her Bible out of the packing boxes and sat down to read, starting with Matthew and on through the gospels. Memories of the stories learned in her childhood Sunday school classes came back and, when Jesus said, "except you come unto me as a little child," she told Him she wanted to be that child.

Maybe there was more to it than that, but she'd never felt such peace and acceptance before in her entire life. Love, that's what it was, plain and simple.

When Mac took her hand, she could scarcely breathe from the love welling up. She hugged Jonah with her other arm, and he leaned against her, a smile lighting his face.

The processional choir started singing at the rear of

the sanctuary and the melody of "Angels We Have Heard on High" led forth up the center aisle and both sides. The altos, tenors, and basses followed, and the music grew on the *glorias* as they drew together in front and sang in full harmony, "in excelsis Deo." They sang the second verse and then flowed up into the choir loft to finish with a swell of the *glorias* again. "In excelsis Deo."

When the final notes ceased in all but memory, a deep male voice from somewhere behind them began. "In those days a decree went out from Caesar Augustus that all the world should be enrolled." The truest story ever told continued until he read, ". . .and she gave birth to her firstborn son and laid him in a manger."

Opposite the adult choir in their burgundy robes, a children's choir sang "Away in a Manger," their voices piping, their faces so serious above their blue robes. Rebecca looked down at Jonah. *Next year, son of mine, you'll be singing with that choir. I'm so sorry I've kept you from this.*

The voice continued with the story from Luke, and the congregation responded with the carols that fit. When the last voice trailed off, a spotlight shone on a soloist. A violin played the opening bars of a song Rebecca had never heard, a piano joined, then a flute, and finally the singer. "Love came down at Christmas, in a baby meek and mild. Love came down at Christmas, a precious holy child." The piano swelled, the violin flowed in, and the flute notes danced on the light.

Rebecca closed her eyes and listened with all her heart. The final lines, "a gift of love, from heaven above. Love came down at Christmas. Love came down to stay."

That's it, the gift of love, so perfect. The gift is what it's all about. She wanted to leap and shout, "It's the gift," to hug everyone in sight. Love beyond description welled from within her, beyond her ability to hold it in. She glanced around, sure that everyone must be feeling what she was feeling. Sensing. Shouting without words. The violin played the last note and it hung in the air like a wondrous fragrance. The lights were extinguished, and a candle was lit at the front and center of the sanctuary. Two others lit their candles from it and, so, the light passed down through the darkness. From the first one in each pew, the light grew. The organ swelled.

Danielle lit her candle and then her father lit his from hers. He turned to Rebecca and, as she tilted her candle to his flame, he took her hand to hold it steady. She looked into his eyes and it was all there. He knew the love. His smile, slow and easy, settled around her heart's abiding place.

She smiled back, a slight nod, then turned to let Jonah light his candle. All passed in a second—but would last forever. The Gift came to be at Christmas.